WITCHES AND WEAVERS AND GHOSTS, OH BOY

A CARY REDMOND SHORT STORY ANTHOLOGY

KAT SIMONS

T&D PUBLISHING

WITCHES AND WEAVERS AND GHOSTS, OH BOY

CONTENTS

For friends and found family.

And to my own family, for having my back.

INTRODUCTION

I started writing short stories for the Cary Redmond series as a way to explore some of the earlier events in Cary's life that I'd alluded to in the novels and wanted to know more about. Writing those stories helped me get to know Cary's closest friends a lot better—as well as letting me indulge in more Cary adventures that didn't have to tie directly into the main storyline.

These three novellas each center one of Cary's three best girlfriends, who all have interesting histories of their own.

The first story in the collection, *Cary vs the Goblin King*, was also the first of the novellas I wrote. I knew Marianne had a history with the goblin king after writing the origin story of her friendship with Cary. And I referenced that history in one of my favorite scenes in book three of the main Cary Redmond series, The Trouble with Leopard Queens and Shifter Wars. In that scene, I made it clear the "real" goblin king is not the sexy hunk that was David Bowie's goblin king in the movie *Labyrinth*—one of my all time favorite classic fantasy movies—and that got me to thinking I really wanted to show the story when the girls all met the goblin king in "real life."

Once I'd written a story centering Marianne, and giving a glimpse into her fantastically interesting life, I knew I wanted to write stories centering Angie and Lucy as well. Lucy's was obvious. I love Hawaii and taking a trip with the girls back to Lucy's home town just seemed a recipe for trouble. In *Cary Goes to Hawaii*, not only does Cary encounter trouble, she has to face one of her greatest fears—ghosts.

Finally, in *Cary and the Demon Witch*, I drop a few more hints about Angie's mysterious background and her dealings with demons. This story was originally published before the first book in Angie's spinoff series, but I wrote it after I'd written book one of the Demon Witch series and had a better idea myself about Angie's past. Which gave me some room to insert things that will…come up in that series.

I very much enjoyed writing these novellas. I love spending time with Cary and her friends, and getting to center each one was a delight. I hope you'll enjoy their stories, too!

Kat Simons
April 2022

CARY VS THE GOBLIN KING

Protectors don't get nights off…

Girls' night means different things to different groups of friends. For Cary Redmond and her three closest friends, it means staying in and watching a classic 80s film while eating Mexican food and drinking margaritas. The perfect evening, with the perfect company…

Until an unexpected guest crashes the party. Literally.

In the ensuing wreckage, Cary discovers her night off has just become a work night. Since she's a magical Protector, she's used to diving in to keep the good guys safe from the bad guys. But this time, it's her dearest friends in danger.

And no one, not even the Goblin King, messes with Cary's friends.

1

Angie shut off the movie and all four women leaned back in her softly cushioned couch and sighed.

"That is a very good movie," Cary said. She'd seen *Labyrinth* before, it was one of her favorite classic fantasy movies. But watching it again with her three best friends, especially when it was the first time for Lucy, had been a great way to spend girls' night.

She, Angie, Lucy, and Marianne had started girls' night just in the last few months, after they'd all met separately, and discovered how well they got along together as a group. It wasn't often you could introduce your friends to other friends and have them all bond so well. Cary had been delighted. And girls' night had become one of her favorite escapes from her workday.

She raised her mostly empty margarita glass, just to celebrate her happiness. "To David Bowie."

The other three raised their glasses too—Marianne was the only one with much left in her glass, though Cary wasn't sure if that was because she'd refilled more recently or been drinking slower.

"To David Bowie," they all said in unison before downing whatever was left of their drinks.

"You know," Marianne said, leaning forward to place her glass gently, and very carefully, on Angie's thick wooden coffee table. "The real goblin king is not nearly that sexy. In fact, he's not even a little sexy."

"That's very disappointing," Lucy said, her little girl voice making the statement sound even more profound.

At least to Cary. But that might have been the influence of the margaritas.

"Not even a little sexy," Marianne said again, and sighed, running a hand over her short, natural curls. "I'm not too proud to admit, if he looked like David Bowie, I would have spent a lot less time resisting his attempts to kidnap me over the last twenty years."

Lucy snorted. "Don't let Gina hear you say that."

Marianne smiled, but the look was wistful. "I don't dare say any of this to Gina."

Marianne's long-time girlfriend was mundane and had nothing to do with the magical worlds. She didn't know Marianne was more than just a seamstress. Marianne was a weaver. She and her two sisters could integrate magic into the clothes they made, and when working together, they could even weave gold. Though Marianne insisted that was the least of her skills. Mostly just a parlor trick.

Unfortunately, it was a parlor trick the goblin king coveted.

When Marianne and her sisters reached adulthood, they'd decided to live apart—even though they were very close—in an attempt to distract and dissuade the goblin king. It hadn't worked completely. The bastard kept coming for them. But the attempts on Marianne had slowed in the last few months. Everyone was pleased with this turn of events.

Cary hadn't met the goblin king yet, just one of his minions. That was how she and Marianne had initially bonded—well that, animals, and all things 80s. They'd known each other before, when Cary had still thought she might be a veterinary technician and had been working at the clinic where Marianne occasionally volunteered. At that point, Cary hadn't known Marianne was a weaver. Though, to be fair, Cary hadn't known the world held things like weavers and goblin kings.

She'd learned all that after rescuing a puppy from a demon and being tricked into becoming a magical Protector.

Lucy groaned and rubbed her face. Her messy red bun slipped sideways on her head. "I have to teach an early class tomorrow morning."

Lucy was the only technically mundane woman in their little group, but she was a multi-blackbelt martial artist who could fell men twice her size. And given her size—tiny wasn't an unreasonable description—that was an even more impressive sight to behold.

She'd taken to their weird world of the supernatural like it was normal, though, and happily settled into the group. She and Cary had also bonded over animal love. And nagging parents. Lucy's dads wanted her to settled down and get married. Cary's mother kept making the same argument. It was a thing, and she and Lucy had spent a lot of time bemoaning the parental pressure.

"I shouldn't have had that last margarita," Lucy said sadly, dropping her hands to her lap.

"Taxis for everyone!" Angie announced and stood to clear the remains of their dinner, a Tex Mex feast of tacos and nachos.

Cary lumbered off the couch to help, snatching a last nacho chip off the tray as she followed Angie into her bright, open kitchen.

"Thanks for hosting girls' night again," she said.

"No problem," Angie said. "I love having you all over. It's nice to have people in the house who aren't clients."

Angie was a witch and psychic who ran a pretty successful psychic's reading business out of her home. She had a front room set aside specifically for her clients, all decked out in dark colors, velvet and silk drapery, a beaded curtain covering the door. Crystal balls and arcane looking paraphernalia scattered about. Outside that room, though, Angie's house was comfortably decorated in a more southwestern theme, a look that better suited her personality.

They were loading the dishwasher when a crash from the other room stopped them cold.

"Oops," Cary said.

They hurried back to the living room, assuming one of the others had dropped a margarita glass.

Only to discover that had not been the reason for the crash.

Cary instinctively hurried to get between Lucy, Marianne, and the very large—she squinted—man sprawled on top of Angie's now destroyed television set.

"Sorry," Lucy said, blowing a lock of hair off her forehead. "He startled me. I'll buy you a new TV."

Angie waved that away. "I have insurance." She scowled at the newcomer. "Though I would like an explanation as to why there's a strange man in my home." Her green eyes narrowed. "Or whatever the hell you are," she muttered.

"Girls," Marianne said with a sigh as the man cursed and scrambled back to his feet. "Meet King Goffin. The goblin king."

2

There was a beat of silence while the newcomer rearranged his clothing and pulled himself up to his full height.

Lucy was the first to break. "Well, that's very disappointing."

"I told you," Marianne said.

The real goblin king did, indeed, bear no resemblance whatsoever to the sexy David Bowie. Not even a little bit.

And Lucy was right. It was surprisingly disappointing.

The real goblin king was tall, taller than Cary had expected actually. He towered over them all—which made Lucy's flipping him over onto the TV even more impressive. But all the height was overwhelmed by the gangly limbs, a seriously hunched posture, and dirty dark hair hanging down over his face. His skin was an interesting shade of green, pale and sort of hard to tell it was green. Mostly he just looked maybe a little sickly. Like the green had too much yellow in it and he was jaundiced. He had a substantial nose and prominent brow but no eyebrows. His jaw was thick. So were his lips, but in a way Cary found a bit off-putting. His eyes were huge for his face, disproportionately huge in his wide features. And while Cary might have expected dark eyes, his were actually a bright bright green.

Almost as bright as her bosses, the North American Fae who created Protectors—she'd nicknamed them the Nags because they were.

The myriad of warts, lumps and bumps covering the goblin king's face and hands were probably considered attractive to other goblins— at least according to Cary's readings; but to be fair, she was still learning so she couldn't say for certain. His fingers were long and tipped with ragged, dirty, but sharp fingernails, curved so that they almost looked like claws. He wasn't wearing shoes, his feet were covered in a layer of dark hair, the nails poking out as raged and sharp as his fingernails.

His clothes were…well, not what Cary might have expected from a *king*. He had pants on. At least, she assumed those were pants. There were a lot of tears and mixtures of texture and material. The same with his shirt, which was vaguely tunic shaped, but it had so many different layers of material, discerning its original intent was impossible.

There were also some bits of metal woven into all of his clothing, though Cary suspected the metal was iron-free. Fae—even goblins— had an allergy to iron. The level of allergic reaction depended on species and individual, but they all had some reaction. Even being inside Angie's house would be intolerable to some of the more sensitive Fae. Obviously, the goblin king wasn't overly sensitive. Cary was no expert, but she thought the metal might be aluminum. It kind of looked like crinkled aluminum foil in some areas.

She wanted to be fair to the goblin king. She felt bad judging his looks by a human standard since, she suspected, for a goblin he was probably pretty handsome. But he was no David Bowie. And after just having seen *Labyrinth,* she was having trouble getting around the contrast.

"Marianne Johnson," he said, his voice surprisingly high and piercing. Given his height and stature—and the thickness of his jaw— Cary had anticipated a deep voice. His squeaking made her wince.

"Your Highness," Marianne greeting him formally. "What the hell are you doing here?"

"I've done my best to convince you to join me voluntarily—"

Marianne snorted meaningfully at that.

"Now, I'm done trying to persuade," he said, ignoring her interruption. "You're coming with me. You will weave for me."

"No," Marianne said, bluntly.

"She's not going anywhere with you," Lucy said.

"You cannot stop me, mortal."

"She *just* tossed you on your ass without even thinking," Cary pointed out, gesturing to the TV.

"She took me by surprise," he said, his voice rising to an even squeakier note. "No mortal would have been able to do that without… without the element of surprise. I am a king! I will have my way."

He actually stamped his foot.

Cary sighed. "So disappointing."

"Right?" Marianne said. To the king, she said, "Listen, Goffin, you've been at this for years. My sisters and I aren't going with you. We aren't your servants and we have no intention of being."

"You have no choice," the king said. His sneer revealed a set of very white, sharply pointed teeth.

He made a gesture with his arm, and what looked like a scepter appeared in his hand. The long bar was made of gold, the rounded top looked like crystal. It was the closest he'd come so far to a David Bowie-esque goblin king. He rolled the scepter across his hand and snapped his arm out in front of him. In the next moment, through a flash of dramatic smoke, more goblins emerged into Angie's living room.

Angie huffed. "I knew I should have activated my circle after he arrived."

Cary glanced back at her.

She shrugged. "I didn't want to trap *him* in."

"Makes sense," Cary said.

The circling goblins were all of various sizes, from the very diminutive, like the little guy sitting high up on one of Angie's bookshelves, to the pony-sized fellow with the cudgel at the kitchen door. Only a few were as tall as Angie's six-foot height. But several were almost as tall as Cary and Marianne. And fewer than Cary would have expected were shorter than Lucy.

There were easily thirty of the bastards crowded into Angie's living room. And Angie's living room, though comfortable, was not that big.

Another crash made Angie scowl. "Hey, you break it, you pay for it," she snapped.

"You are outnumbered." The king laughed. "I will finally have my weavers."

"No," Marianne said again. But she was staring at the circling mass of goblins. To Cary, she murmured, "He's never brought the full court before."

"Guess he's tired of waiting." She reached back and patted Marianne's hand. "Don't worry. You're safe."

King Goffin scowled at Cary. "There are three of you to protect her and thirty of us. You have no chance." He flicked a glance at Lucy. "Even with your...self-defense training."

"Well, now that's just insulting," Lucy said. "I *own* a dojo and *teach* self-defense as well as three different martial arts, you ass. I'm a blackbelt."

"I don't know what that means," he said, his thick brow bunched with his frown.

Lucy let out an exasperated sigh. "Men!" she snapped, flicking her hands up.

Cary shook her head. "She's right, you know. You're being rude."

The king's scowl deepened. "I'm here to take the weaver." He glanced at the other goblins, as if unsure of what he was supposed to say to their comments.

"He doesn't spend much time in the human world," Marianne said. "He doesn't really get what you're saying to him. I was pretty impressed he knew the term 'self-defense'."

"Thank you, Weaver," the king said. Raising his head regally—a look somewhat lost when his crown lilted to one side. "I do try."

"I know you do. But I'm still not coming with you."

"You will. And you will willingly do my bidding."

"No," Marianne said. "You've been trying this for twenty years. It's not happening. Not now. Not ever."

"Take her," he ordered, snapping his fingers at the other goblins.

The lot of them surged forward as one. There was a lot of yelling, and chortling, and shouting, and clash of metal...

And then a lot of cursing and startled screams as they came up against Cary's shield and one-by-one got flung back onto their asses.

Cary shook her head again. "So rude."

"Right?" Lucy said with a harrumph.

"Attack!" Goffin ordered.

Cary and her friends waited them out. All three had seen Cary's Protector shields at work and knew they'd hold off a horde of goblins without too much difficulty. Although she'd been doing this job for a couple of years now, she still didn't know how her shields worked. She just knew if she was standing between a bad guy and a good guy, the shields happened. And they encircled those she was protecting. So the little goblin bastards trying to sneak up behind them weren't having any better luck than the ones charging directly at them. Once she was in place, she could keep everyone safe.

But waiting for bad guys to figure out they couldn't get through her shield was sometimes a little monotonous.

"What should we watch next girls' night?" she asked over the noise. She winced when something else of Angie's broke.

"Damn it," Angie cursed under her breath. "They better not get into my office. I have computer equipment I don't want to have to replace."

"I think we should stick to the fantasy theme and watch *Princess Bride*," Marianne said.

Cary grinned over her shoulder at her. "As you wish."

"Ha!" Lucy laughed. She glanced around. "Though, what I really wish was that these guys would stop trying to kidnap Marianne. It's kind of boring just standing here when you know they can't get through."

"You're free to get out into the mess of them and toss them around some," Cary said. "You can always jump back behind me if they get to be too much."

Lucy scowled at her. "I could handle them."

"Do not get into the middle of this fight," Angie said, her hard gaze leveled on Lucy. "They're doing enough damage on their own." Another loud crash and they all winced as Angie's sturdy wooden coffee table collapsed under the weight of three goblins. "Damn it. I really liked that table."

"I'll help pay for the mess," Marianne said. "Since the dumbasses are here for me."

"It's okay," Angie said with a sigh. "It's just annoying."

"Tell me about it. They've shown up at my place of business a few times now and it's really starting to tick me off."

"Enough!" King Goffin shouted.

His squeaky voice pierced the other noise like a knife and made Cary wince again. The surrounding goblins climbed back to their feet. A lot of grumbling was involved. One of them, a largish fellow with a hooked nose, elegantly coifed blond hair, and very dark eyes, growled at her. Cary shrugged. Not her fault they were the bad guys in this situation. Maybe they shouldn't go around trying to kidnap people.

"You really shouldn't go around trying to kidnap people," Cary said.

"But the children love us," the blond goblin said.

"Ew," Cary said. "Don't let me catch you trying to kidnap kids. I will put my foot in your ass for that."

Technically, Lucy was the "putting her foot in your ass" one of the group. But when it came to defenseless kids and animals, Cary knew she could become a foot-in-the-bad-guy's-ass kind of person. With or without her Protector magic.

"I need the weaver," King Goffin said. "I will have the weaver. Your time is up."

Marianne motioned to the still grumbling goblins. "How, might I ask, do you intend to get me when a small army didn't work?"

"No witch shield can stop me."

"Well, technically, that could be true," Angie said. "But I wouldn't bet against a witch's shield. Mine, as it happens, are pretty good."

"Yeah they are," Cary said to be supportive. At the moment, they weren't using Angie's magic, but she had no doubt her friend could conjure something very useful just then if needs be.

"Weaver," Goffin said, ignoring them. "You will come with me."

"Why do you keep saying that when all evidence points to the contrary?" Marianne asked.

The king's smile widened, showing off his perfect, but very pointy, teeth. "Because I have Eunice already."

3

Silence followed King Goffin's statement.

Eunice was Marianne's youngest sister. As far as Cary remembered, she was living in North Carolina. And because she was the youngest, she was the least useful to the goblin king without the other two sisters. Which meant she'd always had less trouble with him than her two older sisters. Their middle sister, Ginger, lived in Chicago. She dealt with the goblin king's minions occasionally, but still not as often as Marianne.

As the eldest, Marianne had had to fend the old bastard off for a lot longer and a lot more frequently. She said it was because none of the magic the king wanted, none of the gold weaving, worked without Marianne, so he'd always focused most of his attention on her. Which, as far as she was concerned, was for the best. She was very protective of her sisters.

But now that the king had her youngest sister, the game had changed.

"What do you want in exchange for Eunice?" she asked, her voice low.

"You, of course. And your sister. You will weave for me. You will ensure no one has more riches than me. You will make sure I remain king!"

Cary raised her brows. Huh? Wonder what that meant.

"Getting some competition, finally, eh?" Marianne asked, but without her usual smirk. "Without Ginger, we still can't do what you want us to do."

"She's being taken to my realm even now," Goffin said. "She didn't have your witches to help her."

"Well hell," Cary muttered. "What do you want to do?" This to Marianne.

"Seems I have to go into goblin territory and get my sisters back," she said.

Cary nodded. "Okay. I'll go with you."

"Not going without me," Angie said. "I've never been to the goblin realm. Should be fun."

Marianne snorted. "Not as fun as you might think."

"I've got your back, too," Lucy said.

"You are all the best," Marianne said. "But I can't ask it of you. This is my family issue."

"And we're part of your family," Cary said. "Found family counts when it comes to rescuing people from goblin kings."

Marianne smiled. "I love you too," she said quietly.

Cary winked, then face the goblin king. "We're going only as long as it takes to get her sisters out, you know that right? I mean, she's not staying, and there will be no gold weaving."

Goffin smirked. "We'll see." He rolled a glass ball out of thin air, swirling it over one hand as it grew.

He might not look like David Bowie, but that glass ball trick was pretty reminiscent of the trick Bowie used in the movie.

They watched the ball grow until it was large enough to encompass all four of them. But when the king threw it at them, it shattered against Cary's shields. Oops.

"Forgot," she said. "Sorry." To her friends, "I need to stop…uhm… you know, if he's going to take us somewhere. But I'm not sure how to, uh, make it stop without, uhm…" She made a face. She couldn't talk about this aloud without giving too much away.

She was in full Protector mode, and the only way her shields shut down now was after the danger ended, or her friends all step around her, moving out of her protection and facing the bad guys on their own. But she couldn't say that out loud and she was loath to allow it at any rate. Especially when they were going into hostile territory.

She faced the king again. "We need to go voluntarily," Cary said. "Like, through a doorway, not kidnapped in a glass bubble. Got a doorway of some kind?"

"This is the weirdest kidnapping I've ever been to," Lucy muttered.

"Been to a lot?" Angie asked. "If you tell me yes, I'm going to worry about you."

Lucy laughed. "This is my first, if that helps. But it's still hella weird."

"Yeah that it is," Angie agreed.

"That's what you get with goblins," Marianne said.

"Doorway?" Cary asked again. Goffin looked a little confused, so she figured she'd better get him back to the subject at hand.

He opened his palm and another glass ball appeared, like he'd had it cupped there the entire time. The ball moved around his hand without him doing much at all, only very slight wrists movements that Cary could spot, and the glass ball grew. When it reached the size of a basketball, he set it on the floor. He kept his gaze on Cary the entire time. Probably wondering if she'd manage to shatter the glass again.

She was kind of curious about that, too.

The ball vibrated, rolling in a small circle that kept it mostly in one place as it continued to grow until it was the size of the goblin king. Cary had this weird impression of one of those sterile bubbles designed for people with bad immune systems so they could move around better. Then the glass turned opaque, like it was filling with smoke, before filling with utter darkness, and finally blackening completely, so she could no longer see the goblins on the opposite side.

She waited, watching, her eyes narrowed. Goffin tapped the opaque ball twice with the crystal at the top of his golden scepter, a gentle rap, like knocking at a door. And a door at the center of the person-sized ball opened, a rectangular piece of the glass swinging outward.

She nodded at him a moment before admitting, "Okay, that was impressive."

He straightened his shoulders a bit, nodding at one of the goblins she could no longer see behind the ball-doorway.

"Where does this take us?" Angie asked.

"My home," the king said.

"What *part* of your home?" Marianne asked. "'Cause I'm not getting confined in your dungeon with a pile of straw. I want to see my sisters. Immediately."

He made a face, pressing his lips together. "Fine." He tapped the giant ball again. The door swung closed. He tapped three times, and it opened again. Light spilled through this time. Light and the distinct, earthy scent of a peat fire.

"Better?" Cary asked Marianne. "Do we go?"

Marianne pulled in a deep sigh, her gaze on the doorway. "We go."

"Stay behind me," Cary said, taking the lead. She paused at the threshold. "Wait, does anyone need anything before we leave? Bathroom break? Anything?"

"I'm good," Lucy said. Her voice was higher and quieter than normal.

For all her kickass bravery, and acceptance of their weird world, this was, as far as Cary knew, Lucy's first time stepping out of her own realm. She couldn't blame Lucy for the slight tremble in her voice.

"Let me grab my purse," Marianne said. When the goblin king scowled at her, she shrugged. "Habit. Not good to get too far from all your necessary keys and…women's things."

The king nodded as if this made perfect sense and he clearly understood what she was talking about even though it was obvious to Cary he didn't have a clue.

"I'd better grab my keys, too," Angie said. "Just in case."

Cary tried not to smile. She kept her lips pressed together in a neutral line as Marianne grabbed her small leather purse and Angie wove through the goblins to get her keys out of the bowl near the front door. The goblins looked at each other as she passed, their gazes jumping back to their king for signs of what they were expected to do.

The fact that Angie had left Cary's protection to get her keys and none of the goblins took advantage of that was reassuring on several levels—obviously, once Marianne had agreed to go to the goblin realm, they weren't as keen on attacking. But also it was a great sign that they had no idea what Cary was. And if they didn't know she was a Protector, maybe didn't even know what Protectors were, then she had a good chance of not only surviving all this, but getting her friends out alive, too.

Yay for survival!

Boo for the fact that the margaritas had worn off, though. Mostly.

When Angie rejoined them, Cary gave her friends one last chance to back out of this adventure. "Are we all good now? And are we all sure?"

She, Lucy, and Angie all looked to Marianne.

"I'm going through that door to get my sisters," Marianne said, "so yeah, I'm good to go. And I'm very, very sure."

"Okay then." Cary faced the opened glass ball and straightened her shoulders. She peeked through the door, trying unsuccessfully to see beyond the light spilling out.

Walking into the unknown with her three best friends to protect and two missing sisters to rescue.

Just another day in her life as a Protector.

4

Cary squinted against the brightness until she was fully clear of the glass ball's magic door. When the glare cleared, she blinked at her surroundings. In surprise.

"Huh," she said.

"I know, right?" Marianne said from behind her.

"Welcome to my realm," King Goffin said, now standing in front of them as if he'd materialized into the space instead of needing the door.

Which was probably exactly what he'd done.

Cary took in the full impact of the goblin realm again, still...baffled.

It was lovely. Cozy and warm.

The room they'd stepped into resembled a huge wooden hall with a thatched roof. In the center of the space was a huge open fire pit, the peat fire creating enough warmth to saturate the hall without making it stuffy, that lovely peat scent surrounding her now. Mingling with the peat was a warm honey scent Cary couldn't find a source for.

The wooden walls were hung with colorful tapestries, and trinkets in gold, silver, and glass dangled from the thatching and wooden beams overhead. The floor was packed dirt, but it was covered by layers of clean, colorful rugs in a patchwork arrangement that managed to look charming rather than chaotic. Wooden chairs and cushion-covered couches were scattered throughout, and a single long wooden table circled by high-backed chairs took up one whole side of the hall.

The bright lights came from a series of glass globes that seemed to be floating in a line down the length of the hall, casting a perfect brightness over the room—warm and comfortable but not glary. Just the exact right level of lighting for a…home.

There were goblins everywhere, too. Hanging from the rafters. Crowding the couches and chairs. Sprawled across the rugs and on top of the long table. Some seemed to be playing games. Others were contemplating their navels—as far as Cary could tell. The place was piled high with goblins. Yet they all looked perfectly comfortable with the crowded nature of their arrangement.

Cary shook her head. "Not what I was expecting."

Though, to be fair, she wasn't sure what she'd been expecting. A barren landscape and a stone labyrinth maybe?

"Nothing's ever what you expect," Marianne said with a sigh. To the king she said, "Where are my sisters?"

Goffin smiled and waved his scepter. At the far end of the room, two huge glass balls appeared. And inside them, two women.

Two very pissed off looking women.

"King Goffin," one said. "You better release us now. Or I swear to everything holy I will tear you a new asshole."

"That would be Ginger," Marianne said with a fond smile.

Ginger, Marianne's middle sister, was a tall, shapely woman with skin a few shades darker brown than Marianne's and hair substantially longer. Her twists were decorated with little gold clips down the lengths that hung to nearly her hips, and a bundle of the twists were wound on top of her head to create a large bun. She was dressed in casual, loose tan pants and a fitted tank top that showed off her perfectly muscled arms.

Ginger pounded her fist against the glass ball, hard. And to Cary's amusement, the king took a step back.

The woman in the other glass ball looked a bit younger than

Marianne and Ginger, maybe early twenties. She was smaller, too. Both shorter and petit. Where Marianne had generous curves, and Ginger was elegantly well-muscled, Eunice was a wisp. Her reddish-brown hair was straightened and cut in a cute asymmetrical bob, the longer front layers hanging to just above her shoulders. She wore a beautiful orange silk skirt that fell to her ankles and a soft fuzzy white sweater. Her makeup was extravagant and expert, with touches of glitter across her cheekbones and over her lids. And her jewelry was made up entirely of feathers and autumn colored glass beads.

Neither sister was wearing shoes, Cary noticed, and she wondered if that was something the goblin king had arranged or just coincidence.

"Marianne, what are you doing here?" Eunice said. "You know this is what he wants. *You.* You should have stayed away."

Eunice's voice was beautifully melodious, deep and resonant. And more…substantial than her age hinted at.

"I came to rescue you," Marianne said. She gestured to the glass ball prisons. "And from the look of it, you need me. How the hell did you let this man get to you?"

Eunice rolled her eyes and set her hands on her hips, pressing her lips together.

Ginger answered the question. "I don't know about Neecy, but I got blindsided in front of actual mundane humans. Near my place of work, no less." She glared at Goffin. "I'm going to have to find a new job, you sonofabitch. And maybe move cities. And I love Chicago. You have a lot to answer for."

"You three will weave for me now," Goffin proclaimed, waving his scepter.

Laughter and cheers erupted around the hall. Goblins fell over in their enthusiasm. And Cary finally spotted the source of the honey scent. Goblets and goblets of a golden colored liquor she was pretty sure was mead were passed around the hall. Goblins drinking and spilling and generally being rowdy and making a mess.

"You are a sonofabitch," Ginger said again and folded her arms over her chest.

"So," Cary said, leaning back a little and dropping her voice so only her friends could hear her over all the goblin celebrations. "What do we do now that we're here?"

"Break those prisons and walk out with my sisters," Marianne said.

"Two points," Cary said, lowering her voice even more. "I'm open to suggestions about breaking open the prisons. Not sure how to do that myself. Also, how do we leave since the king closed the door back to Angie's place?"

Angie waved that away. "I have that part covered. It's why I needed my keys. Little portal spell. It won't last long so we'll have to be careful about when we use it."

"You can do portal spells?" Cary asked.

"No," Angie said with a grin. "No, this is something a friend from the old days gave me. For emergencies." She glanced around at the mayhem. A half dozen goblins went careening into the long table as they watched and another half dozen seemed to topple over on top of them into a giant bundle of cursing goblins. Angie shook her head. "I think this would qualify as an emergency."

"I need to get my sisters out of those prisons," Marianne said. "We can take care of the goblin horde once we're together, but we have to be together. The glass prisons actually block our ability to work. King Goffin isn't as dumb as he seems."

"But he wants you to work together to make him gold," Lucy pointed out. "How was he going to make that happen?"

"Got me," Marianne said with a shrug. "I've never understood why he thought this would work. But he's been coming for us since Eunice turned five and her weaver powers kicked in. Maybe it's just habit now."

Cary looked around the hall. There were trinkets and knickknacks everywhere. Not just the display hanging from the ceiling, but now that she was paying attention, she noticed them embedded in the dirt floor and filing little alcoves and covering the long table. The place was basically overrun with stuff all tucked into the edges of the larger room.

"Why does he need more stuff?" Cary asked. "What good is gold to a goblin?" She could see a leprechaun wanting to get their hands on weavers. But what was in it for a goblin king?

"Stuff denotes power in their world," Marianne said. "And the more unique, the stranger and more interesting, the better. The king has a dragon scale imbedded inside that scepter of his—a black dragon scale. Pretty rare. The only thing rarer would be a golden dragon's scale."

"Dragons?" Cary asked.

"Like? Real dragons?" Lucy echoed.

Marianne nodded. "They're out there."

Cary had read about them. And how rare they were. Real dragons *and* shapeshifter dragons. Two different species, but they both actually did exist. That had been an eye opening reading session. Fortunately, she hadn't come face-to-face with any dragons so far in her Protector duties.

Though, if she were honest, she kind of wanted to meet at least one. Maybe. If they were in a good mood at the time.

And had already eaten well first.

"The king's black dragon scale ensures he keeps the kingdom," Marianne went on. "No one else has anything to compare to it, last I heard. But there are a few goblins looking to take his throne. Have been for most of my life, so he tells us. And he wants something equally as impressive as his scepter. Three weavers making him gold would qualify."

"Sounds like a stupid way to hold a throne," Lucy said.

"Goblins," Marianne said with a shrug. As if that explained everything.

"So…the prisons?" Cary asked. "Any suggestions?"

"Physical attack?" Lucy asked, eyeing the seemingly delicate glass.

"'Fraid that won't work," Marianne said. "Magic."

Cary remembered Ginger's fist punch to the material and sighed. Magic.

"They're designed for me and my sisters, so nothing in my bag of tricks will work to break them open," Marianne said. "Angie?"

"I can try. But my way will take some time. Building spells against unknown magic gets tricky. Especially without all my gear. It would help if I could get close enough to touch the spheres, sense the magic, feel what it's made up of."

"Okay, well that at least I can arrange," Cary said. "Follow me. Stay behind me." Protector shields away! she thought. Because if she didn't occasionally laugh, she'd probably have cracked by now.

With her friends sticking closely behind her, Cary walked through the throngs of goblins. Once they started moving, all the revelry changed tone. Suddenly there were bodies swarming them. Goblins everywhere trying to reach them.

"What are you doing?" Goffin shouted over the din. "Stop! Stop them!"

More goblins. More mayhem. More bad guys tossed aside.

Cary moved slowly, giving her shield time to adjust to the movement just in case. She wasn't sure it mattered. But given the sheer number of goblins, she wasn't taking any changes.

"Are they multiplying or something?" Lucy asked. "Because there seems to be more than there was just a minute ago."

"Goblins do have a way of doing that," Marianne said with the sigh. "You get one, you get a hundred. And then they're everywhere."

"Like mice. Or ants." Angie tapped Cary's shoulder. "Little more to the left."

Cary thanked her. She couldn't see through the throngs anymore. She was glad Angie had those extra few inches of height to help.

They angled to the left and pushed forward. She kept expecting to accidentally step on one of the littler goblins as they got trampled under the waves of the goblins behind them.

Finally, they reached a space were the goblins were forced to make some room and the glass ball prisons appeared out of the throng. They'd reached Eunice's crystalline prison first.

"I have no idea what you're doing or how you're doing it," she said, "but I like it."

Cary snorted. "Step back a little from the glass, just in case."

Eunice moved to the center of the ball, and Cary turned so she was still between goblins and Angie as Angie approached the glass. After a moment, she muttered something under her breath that sounded like a curse.

"Bad?" Cary asked, keeping her gaze on the still swarming horde. One hit against her shield face first, laughed like it was funny that he'd been flattened against an invisible barrier, then slid to the ground only to be replaced by another three goblins. Cary shook her head.

"A little," Angie said. "It's a pretty strong and complex spell. It's going to take me time to work through it and find the string to pull to unravel it. It's not like ordinary witchcraft. This is Fae magic, and without my books and gear, I'm not even sure I *can* find the thread." To Marianne, she said, "Any suggestions would be welcome."

"They're made to hold me and my sisters," Marianne reminded her. "Nothing I have to bring to the table will help."

"I was hoping you'd had an epiphany," Angie muttered, turning back to the crystal.

"Uhm, I haven't tried this before," Cary said, "but technically, my...powers are supposed to give me the tricks and skills I need in these kinds of circumstances. I could try...something? I don't know."

"Be my guest," Angie said. "This could take me hours to work out. If you have a quicker way to get through these things, I'd be thrilled."

Cary edged closer to Eunice's prison. She set her hand against it even as she kept the goblin throng in her peripheral vision. There was a vibration running through the glass that sparked against her palm and made her skin tingle. The tingling reminded her of how she felt after protecting someone from magic. She pulled her hand away and shook out the tingles.

"You okay?" Angie asked.

"Fine. Just feels a little weird."

"We might want to hurry," Lucy said. "There seem to be even more of these things. And I'm pretty sure I spotted a couple of really really large ones heading our way."

Cary swallowed hard. "Okay, well, I don't know how to unravel a magic spell, but maybe..." She pressed her hands to the glass again. "Eunice, you might want to cover your eyes."

Eunice, frowning at her, tucked her face into her elbow.

"Here goes nothing," Cary said. And she pulled her fist back and threw a surprisingly—to her anyway—accurate punch that landed midway up the sphere. The glass around her fist shattered into a pretty pattern of cracks.

And then it dissolved into soap bubbles.

5

"*U*hm," Cary said into the surprised moment after her punch destroyed Eunice's prison.

Then she rushed forward to pull Eunice into the circle of her protection. Marianne grabbed her sister up in a hug, patting her face to make sure she wasn't hurt. Eunice took the big sister mothering with surprising patience and only a little eye rolling.

"Well that was useful," Angie said. "The blowback made my head hurt. But effective nonetheless."

"That made your head hurt?" Cary asked, wincing.

"You basically brute forced open a containment spell," Angie said. "Everything that can feel magic within a twenty mile radius will have felt that." She glanced at the still intact crystal prison around Ginger. "And they're about to feel it again."

"Any way you can brace your brain against getting hurt?" Cary asked as they pushed forward to reach Ginger.

The goblin swarm increased. Blocking Ginger's sphere from sight. Cary heard the goblin king roar something into the mayhem. She couldn't hear the words over all the laughter and shouting, but he sounded angry. And over all that, she heard—felt?—some heavy steps heading their way. The huge goblins Lucy had warned them about.

"The big guys are coming," Lucy confirmed.

"I'll be okay," Angie said to Cary, answering her question. "Can't avoid the headache of that kind of magical blowback, but it's better than me spending three hours trying to pull a Fae spell apart."

"If you're sure," Cary said.

But they didn't seem to have much choice. The goblin attack increased, getting so crazed, they had to stop their progress for a few minutes while Cary held her ground and kept the masses from reaching her friends. The giant goblins reached them then, huge hands brushing aside smaller goblins, trying to lift Cary's shield off like a platter lid. It didn't work, of course, but watching them try was disconcerting. They were easily eight feet tall and as wide as a truck, and Cary had to crane her neck to see their grinning faces. The grins weren't friendly.

Glass started to shatter around them, though Cary couldn't pinpoint the source. "What the hell is happening?"

She held up an arm to cover her face almost instinctively, because it was really hard not to cover your face when glass shattered right in front of you. She felt a little scratch on her hand and hissed at the sting. If she was going to get hurt, it usually happened when she was jumping in at the start of an attack, before her shields were fully operating. But sometimes, when she dealt with magic, little non-lethal nicks and cuts got through.

Could be worse, she supposed. One little cut, given all the glass shattering around them, seemed a minor blip compared to the potential injuries they could have sustained.

"How are you doing this?" Eunice leaned forward to ask her. "You a witch?"

"I'm the witch," Angie said. She pointed at Lucy. "She's the martial artist."

"Which seems to be a useless skill in this circumstance," Lucy said with a slight snarl.

"You did toss the goblin king on his ass once already," Angie said.

"You did?" Eunice asked. "Wow, I'm sorry I missed that."

"It was a pretty glorious sight," Marianne said. "Even if it did destroy Angie's TV."

"That's what insurance is for," Angie said pragmatically.

Cary kept her mouth shut, though she did smile into her elbow. Her friends had done a lovely job of deflecting Eunice's attention away from Cary's talent. It was just safer for a Protector that way. The fewer people who knew what she was, and what she could do, the better.

"Come on," she said as she sensed a pause in the glass attack. She started edging forward again, pushing gently as they moved forward over the shattered glass. "You suppose there were spells in those?" she asked Angie, glancing down at all the pretty sparkling, deadly sharp glitter under their feet.

"Probably," she said. "Glad I've got shoes on."

Cary, and the others, all stopped abruptly and almost as one looked down at Eunice's feet.

Cary groaned. No wonder the goblins or Goffin or whoever was throwing glass at them.

She was pretty sure her Protector powers extended to their feet because with their first few steps over the glass she hadn't gotten cut, but she did have on substantial hiking boots with thick soles. Marianne was wearing ballet style slipons that didn't have thick soles. Lucy had on tennis shoes. Angie—who had been barefoot in her house—had put on a pair of hiking boots when she'd gone to get her keys.

But Eunice was most definitely going to need a way over all this glass. And Cary wasn't prepared to risk her feet on the off chance the Protector shields would protect them.

Sometimes, not knowing *precisely* how her powers would work in certain situations was a pain in the ass.

"Okay," she said. "I think I can carry you. That'll leave the others free to do damage to the goblins if something goes wrong, and I can still keep you safe."

Eunice gave her a look, then frowned at Marianne.

Marianne shrugged. "Or I could carry you. Up to you. But we're better off not having your bare feet moving across all this glass. Some of those shards are tiny and likely to be tipped with something nasty."

Cary blinked. She'd thought of spells. She hadn't thought of the glass itself having poison on it. She glanced at the small nick on her hand. Her Protector powers should wipe out any poison. If she got really hurt right now, she'd be leaving her charges defenseless and her powers didn't allow that to happen. Still, the realization that her body could be fighting off poison even now was sobering.

She really didn't like the goblin king.

Another series of glass balls rained down from overhead, shattering around her shields and forming a little circle of dangerous glitter around them.

"Don't you have anything in your purse?" Eunice asked Marianne. "I don't want to hamper one of us by having to be carried."

Marianne's purse was a clutch the size of a small paperback book. It was designed to carry a wallet, keys, a lipstick, and a phone. Nothing more. Tailor-made to look pretty with only the bare minimum of practicality. It was not the kind of purse that might have a spare pair of shoes inside.

Except, this was a purse Marianne had made herself. Which made the size of its outer appearance irrelevant.

"No shoes," she told Eunice. "But I do have some really excellent leather."

"That'll do," Eunice said. "Hand it over."

The goblins seemed to redouble their efforts, though a few of them got dragged through the piles of glass. Cary couldn't see what happened to them—there were way too many bodies coming at them in a steady stream now—but there was a lot of screeching and screaming around the laughter and hooting. Some curses in a language Cary didn't know, though the sounds and tone of the words made her certain they were curses.

From her tiny purse, Marianne pulled out a four foot by three foot strip of soft, brown leather. The leather was pliable and thin, not the kind of thing Cary would have considered good foot cover—at least not on the bottom of a foot. Maybe for the top, for a cute pair of boots or something. But the leather didn't look thick enough to do much good against all the glass building up around them.

Eunice took the strip and stretched it between her hands, considering it. She reached out a hand without actually looking at

Marianne, and Marianne set a pair of huge scissors onto her palm. If the leather didn't look like it should fit in the little purse, the scissors most certainly didn't. Eunice proceeded to cut around the leather, first cutting it in half, tucking one half into the top of her skirt while she worked on the other.

Cary couldn't really tell what Eunice was doing. She kept having to look away to pay attention to the goblins. More glass had piled up in front of her and she was starting to worry her own boots weren't going to be enough—her Protector magic better work on that stuff. But every time she looked back at Eunice, the leather had transformed further.

Eunice dropped the first piece to the ground and went to work on the second. When she grunted and handed the scissors back to Marianne to hold, Cary finally took a good, close look at what she'd done to the leather. There on the floor sat a pair of lovely leather boots, not unlike Cary's hiking books. The soles were thick and solid-looking. The tops also a thick brown leather that would come up over Eunice's ankles and looked like it could take a snake strike without giving way.

"Wow," Cary said. Where had the hooks and shoelaces even come from?

"Eunice is the cobbler sister," Marianne said. "Part of her weaver skills make her excellent with shoes. She's made some beauties over the years. I can do decent shoes. We all can. But not like Neecy."

"If you have more leather, I'll make a pair for Ginger as we walk," Eunice said.

Cary could tell she was trying not to preen under her big sister's compliments, but she was smiling pretty big as she took another chunk of leather from Marianne.

Now that Eunice had shoes on, they pushed forward again. Cary hadn't remembered Ginger and Eunice's prisons being this far apart, but the space inside the hall seemed to distort and change as they moved, making it tricky to reach the second prison. Every time she thought she was on the right track, she'd look up and realize the top of the glass ball was actually a few feet in a different direction than the one she'd been heading. It wasn't anything major, not like the prison was suddenly behind them. The shifts were subtle. But after the third time Cary had to correct course, it finally hit her the goblin king was doing this on purpose.

"Damn it," she muttered, angling slightly left. "I can't reach the damned thing if he keeps moving it."

"Now this, I can deal with," Angie said. "He just needs some distraction of his own so he can't focus on twisting our environment around."

"Is that what he's doing?" Cary asked.

"It's his realm. He can do what he wants here for the most part."

That didn't sound good. "Do I want to know what you're going to do?" Cary asked.

Angie grinned. "It'll be fun. Trust me."

Since she did trust Angie, she grinned back and returned to forging a path toward Ginger.

The glass had stopped raining down on them, but the throngs of goblins hadn't ceased throwing themselves at her shields. She was starting to wonder if this had become a game for them. She could swear some of them were purposefully trying to hit the shield at angles that would get them tossed the farthest. There was a lot more laughter now than cursing. And even a few very distinct "woohoo!"s as goblins flew through the air.

Cary shook her head. Goblins were weird.

She heard Angie muttering something under her breath and glanced back once to check on her. She was making some hand gestures and mumbling things Cary couldn't really interpret. Which was pretty typical when Angie was casting a spell, so Cary left her to it. The prison ball seemed to move again, so she edged in the new direction.

Then a faint tingling moved along her skin, a little like the aftereffects of using her Protector magic. And suddenly a series of red balloons starting rising all around the hall. They floated up to the ceiling and then popped, releasing a wash of glitter. More balloons, more glitter.

And the goblins stopped rushing them.

There were actual "ooh"s and "aah"s.

Cary tried not to laugh. The glittered seemed to vanish as it neared the ground, but that didn't stop the goblins from reaching for it. Instead of throwing themselves at Cary, the horde started chasing balloons, racing to get under the glitter showers, climbing on top of each other to grab at the balloons.

The result was no less chaotic, but the chaos was no longer focused on them.

"Cool," Cary said. She frowned at Angie. "But how will this distract King Goffin?"

Angie nodded her chin to the right. "He's got a hall full of disobeying goblins on his hands now. That has to be dealt with first. He can't focus on creating his own illusions until he breaks mine. That gives us about three minutes to reach Ginger."

Across the hall, King Goffin shouted at his horde, tossing his hands this way and that, releasing a series of glass balls that crushed the red balloons. This wasn't working the way he wanted it to, though, because it released the glitter in Angie's illusions and only encouraged the goblins' attention on the balloons.

Lucy laughed. "Goblins are like kids, aren't they?"

"A little," Marianne said. "Really destructive and violent kids."

"But just as distractible," Eunice said.

"More like cats than kids actually," Marianne said.

"Though not quite as independent," Eunice said.

Marianne gestured at the mayhem. "And King Goffin is dealing with the difficulty of 'herding cats' right now."

"This whole place is weird," Lucy said.

"Yeah, it is," Eunice said. "My name's Eunice, by the way." She held her hand out to Lucy.

"Lucy," Lucy said with a grin. "Nice to meet you."

"You two are being way too polite given the circumstances," Marianne said.

"Hey, you didn't bother with introductions," her sister scolded. "Someone has to take care of the technicalities."

Marianne rolled her eyes.

Cary chuckled as she turned back to their path through the hall. They had finally closed the distance to Ginger's prison. Finally!

"What the hell took you so long?" Ginger snapped.

"Goblin king illusions and a horde of the little fuckers," Marianne snapped back. "Stop bitching and let my friend get you out. Stand in the center of the sphere. Cover your face."

"What are you doing? This isn't normal glass."

"My friend isn't a normal woman."

"Aw," Cary said, "thanks."

Marianne patted her shoulder. "You're welcome."

Cary waited until Ginger was a relatively safe distance. Then she once again threw a punch at the glass—or started to before Lucy stopped her.

"You're going to break your thumb punching that way," Lucy scolded. She took Cary's hand and rearranged her fist. "There. Now remember, the power and momentum come from your body, not your forearm."

Cary rolled her eyes. "You do realize that right now none of that will matter, right?"

"But it gets you into bad habits," Lucy said primly. "It's important to get your form right even when you don't necessarily need to have it correct."

Cary shook her head, trying not to grin. This time, Lucy let her finish the punch. And when Ginger's prison shattered, it dissolved into a shower of golden sparks of light, like the release of fireflies across a field.

"I have to give him this," Cary said, "King Goffin knows how to magic up some serious wonder."

"It is his specialty." Ginger stepped out of the circle of sparks and hugged Marianne and Eunice. "Shoes?" she asked when she pulled back from the family greeting.

"I've got you," Eunice said. She handed Ginger the shoes she'd created while they were pushing through the horde.

"Okay," Cary said. "Now what? Home?"

"No!" King Goffin roared over the still cavorting goblins, and silenced the noise in the hall.

6

Goblins who'd just been chasing red balloons and glitter scattered to the side of the hall, making way for their enraged king.

"The weavers are mine," Goffin said as he stalked closer. "I must have that gold."

"No," Marianne said. "To all of that. You keep trying to force us to do for you, and we're not going to put up with it."

"Yeah," Eunice said. "Did it ever, even once, occur to you to just ask for our help? Maybe pay us something for our efforts?"

"That's… That's not how this works," King Goffin said, stumbling over his own confusion. "I demand the weavers make me gold, and you make me gold."

"Wow," Ginger said. "You need to get out more. The world outside Faery hasn't worked that way in… Well, it's been a while now."

"Yeah," Eunice said. "This is modern times, even for weavers and goblins."

"You're going to have to adjust if you want to hold on to your crown," Marianne added.

"And in the meantime," Cary said, "we're going home because my hangover is starting to kick in, and I need a nap."

There was a lot of agreement on that last statement from Lucy and Angie and Marianne.

"Hangover?" Eunice asked.

"We were right at the end of a lovely girls' night, when the king decided to interrupt us," Marianne said.

"Bastard," Ginger muttered.

Marianne crossed her arms over her chest. "Yup."

The king stamped his foot and the surrounding goblins all made "oohing" sounds. One chattered, "You're in trouble now," from somewhere nearby.

Cary braced for an attack, keeping herself and her shields firmly in front of the others. The king's face had turned a funny shade of red-green as his anger built, and his eyes were starting to glow.

The ground beneath them rumbled. The goblins backed farther away, leaving Cary's group in a wide circle of isolation. Nothing happened for a long moment but that ominous ground shifting.

And then a waterfall of bubbles rained down on them. Bubbles, Cary realized by the way they sizzled the rugs just outside her shield, made of acid.

Ah. That wasn't a good thing at all.

"If I can't have you," King Goffin roared, "you will all die!"

The stench of corrosive acid burned in Cary's nose as the deadly bubbles swarmed the area. Goblins raced away from the shower, climbing into rafters and up on tables as the bubbles spread over the floor.

"What now?" Lucy shouted over the shrieks and hisses of the goblins, and the king's screechy laughter.

"Don't move out from behind me," Cary said, "whatever you do."

The women all clumped closer together, moving into a circle with their backs to each other as they watched the splatter of acid. A ring of melted and sizzling rock surrounded them, showing the edge of Cary's shield about two feet out.

Not far enough, Cary thought as she watched the rugs and dirt beneath melt, turning glassy as it cooled. She'd have felt better with a bigger gap between her and all that acid.

Acid. The goblin king was raining acid on them. How horrible did you have to be to have this kind of a temper tantrum over not getting your way?

Apparently, pretty horrible. Cary winced when one slow-to-move goblin got caught in the splash of a bubble. The goblin screamed, a noise that pierced the hall, as he melted into a pile of goo.

Ah, man. Cary covered her mouth and nose. The stench was bad enough—so bad she couldn't even describe it, though she knew it would show up in her nightmares—but now she wanted to protect the goblin horde from their own king.

Marianne reached back and gripped Cary's arm. "He would have happily roasted and eaten you," she said. "Don't feel sorry for the goblins."

"Eaten?" Cary asked without looking back at Marianne. She was still staring at the smoking, green-black goo pile that had been a goblin a moment ago.

"Yeah. They might seem funny and harmless sometimes, but they are not. Don't confuse them for the loveable puppet characters in *Labyrinth*."

"Gross," Cary muttered.

"They'll eat each other, too," Ginger said. "Goblin life is pretty cutthroat."

"I'm not sure that makes me feel any better," Cary said. She still wanted to keep them safe from the acid. She couldn't help it. Her instinct to protect things in trouble was a really irritating character flaw.

But if she tried to save goblins from their own king, she might put her friends in more danger, especially if the goblins decided they needed a snack—so gross!—so she stayed where she was and waited out the king's tantrum.

A second rain of bubbles joined the acid bubbles. Black bubbles this time that seemed to suck in light. They were hard to see, only showing up as a translucent, greenish-tinged shadow against the acid bubbles' glow. But when the black bubbles popped, they seemed to gobble up everything around them.

Cary blinked. Black hole bubbles? That was…bad.

She watched her shields warily. She wasn't sure if the black bubbles were really creating mini-black holes, but they were certainly sucking in all the surrounding bubbles and acid and, once, to her horror, a smallish goblin. The goblin only had time for one quick, panicked screech before it vanished into the blackness. Then the blackness winked out.

When the black bubbles didn't suck up parts of her shield every time they popped against it, her relief made her knees wobble. At least, she was pretty sure they weren't breaking open the shield. The acid bubbles that dropped right behind them still got stopped far enough away that she and her charges were safe.

Still, it was a nerve-wracking thing to watch and she found herself moving back closer to her friends, hoping to create more space between her and the edge of her shield. The others did the same, all of them clumping together tightly, back-to-back, watching the destructive rain.

Silence stretched as Cary's tension tightened in her gut.

The hall seemed emptier now. Whether that was because a lot of the goblins had fled or because they'd been made acid goop or gotten sucked into the black bubbles she wasn't sure. She didn't want to think about it too closely, so she chose to believe they'd been smart enough to run away.

Holding the idea in her head that the goblins had been smart without her brain snorting in disbelief wasn't an easy task.

She kept expecting a third or fourth type of bubble to appear, and the anxiety of waiting to see how the king might try to kill them next made her shoulders ache. So when the bubbles, all of them, finally stopped dropping, Cary couldn't relax or feel even a little relief. She was too busy worrying about what would happen next.

King Goffin stalked toward them, his scepter held low, the crystal orb that topped it pointed at them, at her specifically.

"What are you?" he hissed. "Why can't I kill you?"

"Uhm," she said.

She was usually better with the comebacks, but something about watching goblins turned to goop by acid had robbed her of her usual smartass banter. Probably for the best. That banter did tend to cause more trouble—even if it was fun and pissed off the bad guys so they weren't very strategic about their attacks.

That had been an interesting lesson she'd learned in the last few months. The more pissed off a bad guys were, the more irrational they were. They talked more—bad guy monologuing was *actually* a thing—and they made stupider moves. Normally, that worked in her favor, so she'd been using the smartass-banter technique a lot more lately.

But at the moment, coherent comebacks had abandoned her. Watching the raging goblin king approach was terrifying, and she didn't have the spit to speak, nonetheless issue snark.

The king seemed to grow bigger with each step he took, rising above them now so tall his head brushed the ceiling of the hall.

"Uhm," she muttered again.

"This is pretty bad, huh?" Lucy said.

"Not good," Marianne agreed.

"We should probably leave," Angie said.

"He'll just follow. Even if we can get out," Ginger said, her voice a lot quieter and less angry now.

"Guess he's finally lost his patience," Eunice said, also quietly.

"You have made me very angry," Goffin roared as he leaned down over them and slammed his scepter against the top of Cary's shield.

Cary winced, expected to feel something. When she didn't, she let out a very quiet breath. She'd been doing this job for two years now, and she had learned to trust the Protector magic to be there when she needed it. But sometimes, like now when a giant, enraged goblin was leaning over the top of her, she worried about how much the shields could actually take.

Apparently, enraged goblin kings were not beyond Protector magic abilities, and for that she was extremely grateful.

The king slammed his scepter against her shield again, whipping it against the side of the shield like a baseball bat. The noise of it reverberated through her bones.

"I'm open to suggestions on how we get out of this," Cary said.

Being restricted to a purely defensive talent did have its drawbacks. One of the biggest was she couldn't ever make the bad guys go away. She just had to wait them out. Or talk them into leaving.

She stared up at the crystal head of the scepter as it smashed against her shield again. She wasn't talking this particular bad guy into leaving.

"I've been trying to avoid this," Marianne muttered.

"Are you sure?" Ginger said. "There's a reason we haven't done this before now."

"He's not leaving us any choice," she said. "He's pushed it too far this time."

Eunice sighed loudly. "If he'd just taken the hint."

"Uhm, does this mean you have a plan?" Cary asked, still watching the scepter. It had grown with the king. The crystal ball topping it was now the size of those two-seater Smart cars. The Smart car might be small for a car, but it was huge for a crystal ball. Especially when that car-sized ball kept swinging toward her head. At speed.

"We can give him what he wants," Marianne said.

"Is this like that warning to be careful what you wish for," Lucy asked, "because you just might get it?"

"That would be the one," Eunice said.

"Why have you been avoiding this?" Cary asked, glancing away from the angry giant goblin long enough to look Marianne in the eyes.

"He's not going to like what he gets," Marianne said with a sigh. "And it will leave the goblin realm in chaos for a bit."

"Goblins in chaos, without a leader, are dangerous," Ginger said. "The process of another king rising to power and corralling all that mayhem is…"

"A process," Eunice finished for her.

"Will it spill into our realm?" Cary asked.

"Hopefully not," Ginger said.

"Hopefully? That's all you've got for me. Hopefully?"

Marianne sighed. "You see why we've been trying to avoid this."

"Any other options?" Cary asked.

The sisters exchanged a look. It wasn't a hopeful look.

Cary glanced at Angie. "You have any alternatives?"

Angie glanced up at the giant goblin as he roared and shook the scepter over his head. The move shattered parts of the ceiling. Chunks of thick wood and thatching thumped down around them, making the ground shake.

Cary put a hand up to block the falling debris even though none of it got too close to them. It was hard to watch a roof falling on you without ducking and trying to cover your head, though. Lucy made the same head-covering gesture, then winced and shrugged at Cary as if embarrassed she hadn't trusted Cary's shields.

Since Cary had done the same thing, she could hardly be offended.

Overhead, the night sky was bright and star speckled, with faint wisps of gray clouds streaming by in a breeze Cary couldn't feel inside the hall. Fresh-scented air spilled into the now open building, clearing the fire and peat smells away, but leaving behind the still pervasive scent of goblin. A full moon rose over the broken edges of the roof to cast jagged shadows across the hall. All but two or three of the floating light globes had shattered when the roof fell, and the moonlight wasn't enough to fully illuminate the interior, leaving the hall in a shadowy darkness that hid whatever might still be taking refuge in the far corners.

Angie straightened from her own automatic duck and shook her head up at the goblin. "Nothing I can do with my magic that will stop him from continuing to come after Marianne and her sisters," she said.

Cary looked at Marianne. "Will this stop him for good, what you're about to do?"

"Yes." She sighed. "It'll stop him but good."

"Do I want to know?"

"You'll see."

"How long do you need?"

Marianne looked at her sisters, then assessed their surroundings. To Ginger, she said, "You can do something with the thatch?"

Ginger set her hands on her hips, her lips pursed as she studied the felled bits of straw and grass and other things that had made up the thatched roof. She nodded. "I'll make it work."

"Okay." Marianne reached into her purse and pulled out a thick green piece of silk that she gentle laid out flat on the packed earth. As she worked, she said, "Angie, Lucy, if you could please collect as much of that fallen thatch as possible and hand it to Ginger. Ginger, you're combing. Eunice, you'll need to knit. We don't have time for the loom."

"Shame," Eunice said, "but I've got this." She reached into a pocket Cary hadn't even realized she had in her skirt and pulled out a couple of long, golden knitting needles.

After getting the large rectangle of silk just as she wanted, Marianne grabbed a handful of material from the center and slowly lifted upward. As she did, the silk seemed to take shape, appearing to fall around something solid underneath. With a flourish any stage magician would envy, Marianne whisked the silk aside to reveal a beautiful spinning wheel made of a light-colored wood, the metal parts a darker brass. The wheel seemed to gleam from some internal light in the middle of the now darkened hall.

The goblin king finally stopped raging and roaring. Silence descended.

Cary risked a glance up.

He stared, his huge green eyes glowing in the faint light that came from the wheel. "You are going to spin," he said, his voice still incongruously squeaky, despite his size.

"Cary," Marianne said, ignoring the king, her full focus on setting up her spinning wheel, "I need you to give us time. Keep him from interfering."

"That I can do," Cary said. She'd never even seen a spinning wheel in real life before. She wouldn't have a clue how to help Marianne and her sisters. But she could stand in between them and the king and keep them safe while they worked.

She glanced back up at the still enormous goblin hovering over them.

Boy, she hoped this worked.

7

____

Cary kept one eye on the hovering giant goblin and one eye on the sisters as they started to work. She'd never seen Marianne do her magic before, only gotten the benefits of that magic in some of her clothing—thank Marianne for magic pockets or Cary would never keep a set of keys for longer than a week.

As Marianne settled at her spinning wheel, sitting on a small stool in front of it and ensuring the various bits were in place, Ginger produced two wooden blocks topped with a tight collection of spikes from her pants pockets.

Cary shook her head in awe. The things they hid in their magic pockets…

Ginger handed the blocks to Angie to hold while she took some of the scrap thatch from Lucy. She proceeded to run the material through her hands, bending and folding and breaking it apart.

King Goffin paced a few yards away, watching them closely, his scepter sweeping an impatient arc as he stalked back and forth in the now ruined hall.

Since he was keeping his distance, Cary was able to focus more on what Ginger did with the thatch. After she'd pulled it through her hands multiple times, she had Angie hold the blocks up. Then she slapped the thatch repeatedly through the spikes, combing it, but roughly, until what was left in her hands was a clump of smooth, silky blond strands.

"Wow," Cary said. "You got that from thatch? I didn't even know that was possible."

"This part takes magic," Ginger said, her focus on the material. "The process usually takes a lot longer, requires a single plant material instead of the mixed bag you get with thatch, and entails a lot more steps. But we don't have the time for that now."

Cary's gaze jumped to the goblin king, his impatience palpable. No, they didn't have time for a long process.

After Ginger had one handful of silky strands combed, she handed the mass of formless pale yellow material to Marianne.

Marianne got her wheel spinning with a gentle push, then pumped the petals beneath it in an easy rhythm that kept the wheel spinning fast. She worked the material between her fingers, feeding it onto a thread already fastened to the bobbin. As the material passed through her fingers, it began to shine, the yellowish color brightening. By the time the material had spun into a thread and rolled over the bobbin, it was a bright, glittering gold.

Cary's eyes widened. Gold. They were actually spinning gold. Right before her eyes. "Wow," she said aloud.

"Parlor trick," Marianne muttered.

"I have to do parlor tricks sometimes with my clients," Angie said. "This is a pretty impressive one."

"Yeah it is," Lucy said.

Marianne pressed her lips together but didn't stop turning the spinning wheel. As she neared the end of one mass of rough silk, Ginger handed her another batch. This went on until the bobbin was full of golden thread.

Cary could swear they got more thread spun than they should have given the amount of material they had to work with. But since she'd never even seen anyone spin thread or yarn, she didn't have a clue if this was magic or just an ordinary part of the process.

When the bobbin was completely filled, Marianne stopped the

wheel, removed the thread and handed the whole thing to Eunice. Eunice set the cylinder on its side between her feet, pulling a strand of gold thread up with her as she stood. Wrapping the thread around her finger, she began shifting it through and around the knitting needles.

Cary didn't knit either, so the whole thing looked like a blur of clicking needles and steadily flowing thread to her. But as she watched, a swath of golden material began to emerge under the working needles, slowly growing longer and longer as Eunice seemed to knit faster and faster.

Eunice's expression was focused entirely on the emerging clothe, a growing rectangle of tightly knitted material that looked like the start of a scarf. The cylinder of thread rolled back and forth against her feet, releasing a steady line of finely spun gold. In moments, the small square of material grew long enough to look like a finished scarf. Cary was sure that wasn't normal. There was definitely magic there.

She turned back to the goblin king. He had allowed himself to return to his normal size, tall and gangly but at least no longer a terrifying giant of a being. His eyes gleamed as he watched the material beneath Eunice's knitting needles grow longer.

And longer.

A lot more than Cary thought should have been possible from the amount of thread available.

More magic.

Marianne might call all this a parlor trick, but Cary was still awed. What the sisters could do was nothing shy of amazing.

As the bobbin gave up its last inch of gold thread, Eunice finally reached the end of her work, tying off the ends of the material in a practiced move Cary couldn't follow. But when she was done and slipped the needles out of the clothe, a finished and complete length of golden material draped from her fingers and pooled at her feet, the gold so finely woven, Cary couldn't see the tiny stitches. It looked like silk.

"Wow," Cary said again.

"Holy hell," Lucy murmured. "That was…"

"Yeah," Angie agreed.

"You all are impressed by the smallest shit," Marianne said with a huff.

She stood from her wheel and the sisters gathered together, standing shoulder to shoulder with Eunice in the center, holding the mound of gold silk.

"There is nothing like this in all of your realm," Marianne said, gesturing to the product of their work. "Nothing. It is the most unique thing here. We've never made this before. It doesn't exist outside of this piece."

"It's yours," Ginger continued. "Free and clear. To possess and show off."

"But beware," Eunice said. "It comes with a price."

"Everything comes with a price," Marianne said.

"And to keep it and wear it will cost," Ginger said.

"Maybe more than you are prepared to pay," Eunice said.

"I will have it," Goffin said. "It is mine. There is no price too high! No one in my kingdom will be able to deny I'm the king. It is mine."

Eunice stretched the material out toward the king as he stalked closer, his gaze locked on his prize. He came up against Cary's shield with a face smooshing suddenness that startled them all.

"Oops," Cary said. She reached out to Eunice. "Better let me hand that over." She wasn't sure how to get her shield out of the way to let Eunice hand off the silk because the king was still a threat.

"It must be handed over by the weavers," Marianne said. "It's the bargain."

The way she said bargain made Cary think there was more to this process than she knew. More maybe even than the king realized.

Together, the sisters moved forward, stepping in front of Cary at Marianne's silent gesture. Cary had to fist her hands to keep from objecting. Once they moved outside of her protection, they were vulnerable to attack. Even if she'd be able to get between them and harm pretty quickly, it still went against her instincts to leave them in danger.

They moved as one to stand before the king. They each took up a piece of the silk, so that the gold length was held between them as they presented it.

King Goffin, his expression intent, snatched the cloth from them in a lightning move that made Cary startle. He held up the silk, his eyes wide, his smile triumphant.

"Mine," he murmured.

He made a tossing gesture with the scepter and it vanished into thin air. Then he ran the gold material between his hands, over and over, studying it.

"You will make me more," he said, without looking at the sisters. "I will have more of this. Much much more."

"You've bargained for this," Marianne said.

"And only this," Ginger said.

"More will cost more," Eunice said.

"You do not have enough to pay," Marianne said.

"You've bargained for our release," Ginger said.

"And to go back on that will also cost," Eunice finished.

"I will have more!" the king roared.

The sisters didn't even flinch.

Cary wasn't so sanguine. She started forward, to get between them and the king, but Angie stopped her.

"They've got this," she said quietly.

There was a glow around them now, a sort of golden halo that lit them up like they were made of magic. Cary was reminded of tales of gods and goddesses from ancient myths. Awe overwhelmed her protective instincts. They didn't need her protection. Angie was right. They had this.

King Goffin held up his length of gold clothe and shook it, before wrapping it around his shoulders, like a cloak. Cary blinked when she realized the rectangle of material she'd seen Eunice knit, the piece that *had* looked like a very long scarf, was now the proper length and size to be a cloak. Where the king brought the ends together around his throat, the material twisted by itself into an elegant knot to hold the cloak in place.

Cary blinked. Wow, could Marianne and her sisters do some cool stuff with clothe.

When the cloak was in place, the king straightened to his full height, towering over the sisters. He glared down at them, his expression fierce, his eyes glowing, his jaw tight.

In his squeaky voice, he said, "Make me more. Now. Or I will kill your friends."

Cary very deliberately stepped in front of Angie and Lucy. No one was killing anyone on her watch.

Marianne smiled up at the king. It wasn't a pleasant smile. "Greed will kill," she said.

"Greed will steal," Ginger said.

"Greed will take everything from the greedy," Eunice finished.

With each phrase, the glow around the sisters grew. The halo so bright now it made Cary squint. They illuminated the night, stars in the darkness.

"Greed will kill."

"Greed will steal."

"Greed will take everything from the greedy."

They repeated the three phrases, as if repeating a spell. Over and over.

"Stop saying that," the king roared. "I will have my gold. I will have my gold!"

"Yes," Marianne said. "You will."

The king raised his hand as if to strike out at the sisters, but paused in mid-motion to stare up at his hand.

Lucy gasped. Cary blinked.

"Oh shit," Angie murmured.

8

In the glow the sisters created with their magic, Cary gaped at King Goffin's hand. It was gold. Not just in color, though the color swept across his skin first. But physically, solidly. His hand was gold. His fingers, then his palm, changed before their eyes.

And the change didn't stop there. The gold dripped down his arm, like candle wax, encompassing his wrist, his forearm, rolling down toward his shoulder.

What was left in the wake of the melting drip was a golden limb as solid as any statue's. The king tried to lower his arm and screeched when he couldn't.

"What's happening? Stop it. Stop it!"

"You asked for this," Marianne said.

"You wanted more," Ginger said.

"You broke your bargain," Eunice said.

"And brought this on yourself," Marianne finished.

"All the gold," Angie murmured.

"This is so creepy I think I might throw up," Lucy whispered.

Cary knew the feeling.

Goffin screamed as the gold encompassed his chest, blending with the golden cloak before working up his throat and down his torso. His scream strangled and then cut off abruptly as the gold rose over his jaw. His eyes wide and panicked, he scrambled with his still normal hand at the cloak around his neck, trying to remove it, until that arm too was overwhelmed by the creeping gold.

"I can't watch," Lucy murmured.

Cary didn't want to watch either, but she couldn't look away. Inch by inch, the goblin king turned to gold, a horrible statue of terror.

"Ew," she said.

"Don't mess with the Johnson sisters," Angie said.

"Is it over?" Lucy asked.

Cary reached back and gripped her hand. Lucy held tight. Cary felt as shaken as Lucy sounded. And for a long moment, she couldn't say anything as she stared at the statue that had once been the goblin king.

"Is he dead?" she finally asked Marianne.

"No," Marianne said. "It's the worst part of this spell."

"He's encased but alive," Ginger said quietly. She sounded tired.

"There's more than one reason we haven't wanted to do this," Eunice added, her tone sad. A tear crept down her cheek. "The old asshole brought it on himself, but still…"

"It's a pretty horrible consequence," Marianne finished.

They all fell silent, starting at the king. Knowing his was alive in there, a living statue of gold, made Cary's stomach turn.

"Can you break the spell?" she finally murmured to Marianne.

"No. It's permanent. Well, he might be able to break it eventually. But it will take a full change of his very soul and heart. A true repentance for his greed."

"I'm not sure the old bastard has that in him," Ginger said. "Greed and covetousness are the very traits that made him capable of becoming king of goblins."

"So… Permanent then," Cary said.

"Likely," Marianne said, shaking her head. "Stupid."

Movement around the dark edges of the ruined hall caught Cary's attention. She motioned Marianne and her sisters back behind her, so she could protect them again. Slowly, goblins crept from the shadows, easing forward toward their king.

"We should probably leave now," Cary said.

The murmurs were hard to interpret but there was a lot of goblin chatter as they approached the golden statue. Cary expected outrage, expected them to attack her and her friends at any moment.

What happened next was infinitely worse.

The goblins hooted and cheered and leapt around the golden statue that had been their king, pulling at it, knocking it over and dragging it back and forth, fighting over it.

"Oh god, are they trying to pull it apart?" Lucy asked.

"Yup," Marianne said. "They'll all want a piece of the gold."

"What happens now?" Cary asked.

"They'll fight and rage and try to tear him up," Marianne said. "They'll be in chaos until one rises strong enough to replace the king. And the chaos will be violent and bloody."

One of the raging goblins looked in their direction, a gleam in his narrowed, dark eyes as he stared at the sisters.

"Yeah, we should really leave now," Cary said.

"You're up, Angie," Marianne said.

"On it." Angie reached into her pocket and pulled out her keys.

Cary didn't know what a portal spell might look like when resting on a keychain. But for some reason, she was a little surprised it was a key. A relatively ordinary looking key at that. It was silver and had a slightly large pentagonal head covered in green plastic. Angie held the key between her hands for a moment, then turned and hunted the area just behind them.

"Ah," she murmured. "There."

She ran her hand around the air, then patted it as if she'd found something. With one finger, she traced out the shape of a large rectangle, a faint green glow remaining in the wake of her finger. Then she inserted the key into a spot at the very center of the rectangle, a lock Cary couldn't see. A brief flash, and the faint green rectangle solidified into a dark glowing green line. There was a clicking sound, and the air inside the green rectangle dissolved, melting into the ground and revealing Angie's living room beyond.

"Now that's a cool parlor trick," Marianne said.

"You gotta love magic," Lucy agreed. She glanced over her shoulder at the goblins just as one charged them and smashed up against Cary's shields. "Though, I think the consequences of having access to magic might be a pain in the ass."

"Truer words," Angie murmured as more goblins charged at them. "Let's go. This will only last so long."

Marianne hurried her sisters through first, following close on their heels. Lucy next. Angie waited until Cary stood beside her, then they went through the doorway together. Cary continued to stand in front of the doorway, between her friends and the goblin realm. The goblins that weren't still tearing at their golden king rushed the doorway, and she didn't want any of the little bastards to get through.

Angie held up the portal key, murmured a thanks, and bent the metal in half with surprising ease. Abruptly, the portal collapsed, circling to a central point and then winking out of existence, leaving them once again in Angie's—worse for wear after the attack—living room.

The last thing Cary saw before the portal closed was the golden face of the goblin king as more of his former horde swarmed over him. She shuddered and turned away from the memory of his wide gold eyes.

Angie stared at the mess made of her cozy living room and sighed.

"We'll help you clean up," Lucy said, patting her shoulder. "Not exactly the sort of girls' night we normally have, huh?"

"Yeah. Which is probably for the best." Angie gestured at her scratched wooden floor and the deep gouges in the rug under her flattened coffee table. "I'm not sure my insurance company would approve."

"I'll help you get the place back into shape this week," Marianne said. "I know a great handyman. He can do anything. He helped Gina and I redo our kitchen last year. Very reasonable price, too."

Angie smiled and gave Marianne a hug. "Thank you. It was worth the mess to rescue your sisters, though."

Marianne pulled back from the hug and looked at them all. "Thank you. All of you."

"Sorry we couldn't get out of there without you having to make the king gold," Cary said.

Marianne sighed and exchanged a look with her sisters. "It's done now." She narrowed her eyes. "But we do have to see about getting you two home. I don't suppose you have any i.d. or money on you?"

Ginger reached into her pocket and pulled out a small change purse made of woven strands of silk. "I'm good."

Eunice winced. "I'm wearing the wrong skirt."

Cary wanted to ask how Eunice's skirt had given her access to knitting needles but not her wallet, but she figured after all the young woman had been through, answering Cary's nosey questions was really the last thing she needed.

"You can stay with me and Gina until we can get your i.d.," Marianne said. "Not the first time we've had to do this." She smiled, but there were tired creases around her eyes.

"What do you say?" Angie spoke into the following silence. "Girls' night do over? This Friday. We'll celebrate the genius that is the *Princess Bride* over some Thai food?"

"Perfect," Lucy said.

"I'm in," Marianne agreed, her smile more genuine.

"Thai food and Inigo Montoya? I'm here," Cary said.

"Greatest swordfight every put on film," Lucy said emphatically.

"Can you do any of that?" Cary asked.

As they did their best to clean up Angie's wrecked living room, Lucy regaled them with stories of an exhibition swordfight between two masters she'd seen in Japan. Cary studied her friends, watching their expressions lighten as they chatted, watching the haunted looks fade slowly from Marianne and her sisters' faces. And her own tension finally relaxed around the time Angie's kitchen clocked announced it was three in the morning.

That had been one hell of a girls' night.

CARY GOES TO HAWAII

All vacations are not created equal…

And as far as magical Protector Cary Redmond is concerned, going to Hawaii with her best friends ranks at the top of the list. No work, no magical Protector business, no jumping between good guys and bad guys to keep good guys safe. For two whole weeks. She gets to enjoy sun, sea, and tropical breezes without any paranormal chaos. Couldn't get any better than that.

Except Cary's life bends toward chaos, no matter what she tries. And when paranormal danger rears its head, Cary has to answer the call. Even if it means facing one of her greatest fears.

Because her best friend's future is on the line.

1

Cary stepped out of the jetway into the airport and pulled in a deep breath. Wow.

Honolulu International was a bustling airport, with people from around the world brushing past. The accompanying noise of so many people talking at once came in multiple languages. Bright sunshine spilled in through huge windows, and actual palm trees did sway outside in the breeze. But what Cary couldn't get over was the smell. Humid and fresh and a little salty and definitely full of flowers.

"This place smells great!" She faced Lucy and grinned.

"Nothing like the smell of Hawaii," Lucy said on a sigh, her little girl's voice soft. "Home."

"Do they, like, pump in the flower scent or something?" she asked as she, Lucy, Marianne, and Angie dragged their carry-ons toward the baggage area.

"Whatever they do, I like it," Marianne said, her dark eyes wide as she scanned her surroundings.

This was her first trip to Hawaii too, and she and Cary had been excitedly texting back and forth for the last two weeks about what clothes they should pack.

Lucy's fathers were renewing their vows, and because they wanted to meet all of Lucy's Portland friends, they'd extended invitations to Cary, Marianne, and Angie for the big event. Not a single one of them entertained the idea of saying no to that invitation.

Because Hawaii.

While Marianne and Angie owned their own businesses and could get the time off with just a little prior scheduling, Cary'd had to clear things with her bosses first. Being Portland's resident magical Protector meant she couldn't just run off on a holiday willy nilly. There were *always* people to protect, and she didn't get a lot of down time in her job. Since becoming a Protector, she'd gone to New York a few times to visit her younger sister and her sister's family. The Nags— Cary's bosses—didn't argue too much with her then because it was family. She'd left Portland to visit her parents too, although they lived just up the coast, only a three hour drive away, so that wasn't too far. Easy to drive back if her bosses needed her for a big job.

They'd balked at letting her go to Hawaii, though, since there was an ocean involved.

She'd pointed out that at any other job, she'd get regular vacation time off. They pointed out that she had plenty of time off when she wasn't protecting people. She reminded them that they'd tricked her into the job in the first place, the least they could do was give her two weeks off. They denied tricking her. She said this was one of her best friends. They claimed that wasn't the same as family. She argued strongly that it absolutely *was* the same thing as family. Her faery mentor Jaxer had insisted she'd been working hard and deserved a break. Cary had whined a little more. And finally, the Nags relented.

Now Cary was in *Hawaii*!

"This is just the way it smells here," Lucy said as they wove around a large group of Japanese tourists and another group of older people discussing the cruise ship they were headed for. "And this is just the airport. Wait until you get to the windward side of the island where my dads live." She grinned.

"Why did you move again?" Marianna asked.

"I like seasons," Lucy said, sounding both pragmatic and philosophical all at once.

Cary's gaze caught on a shop with boxes of chocolate macadamia nuts stacked high and her stomach rumbled. "We're getting food, soon, right?"

"Yes, please," Angie said, her tone urgent.

The food on the plane hadn't been bad or anything. They all ate the meal—and it was nice actually getting one. But still, something that wasn't airplane food seemed important right now. And if it involved macadamia nuts, Cary wouldn't object.

"I've got a treat for you after we get over the mountains," Lucy said. "I'm taking you to a Hawaii staple. Zippy's!"

Cary exchanged a look with Marianne and they both glanced at Angie. "Is this a good thing?" Cary asked.

Angie was the only one of them—besides Lucy, of course—who'd been to Hawaii before. She'd only been once, but that still made her the authority—besides Lucy, of course.

Angie shrugged. "I didn't go to Zippy's last time. I did have an excellent plate lunch, but I can't remember where I was for that."

"Oh, I'll get you good plate lunch, too, don't worry," Lucy said. "And my dads' reception will have all kinds of yummy local food." She looked at Cary and frowned a little. "It's a shame you don't like fish. The fresh fish is to die for."

Cary shivered. "Even fresh will not make me like fish."

Lucy took care of the rental car while Cary, Marianne, and Angie collected the suitcases.

As they waited beside the luggage carousel, Cary got a tiny tingle along her spine, a little shimmer of awareness of…something. Usually that meant something to do with her job was about to happen. Either she needed to protect someone, or her bosses were about to show up. But they'd claimed they'd leave her alone on this trip. They'd actually been pretty insistent that they *wouldn't* be coming to Hawaii to disturb her.

She glanced around the luggage area, at all the ordinary humans coming and going, hauling bags off luggage belts, and talking way too loudly. Nothing unusual. Nothing stood out.

No one in trouble.

Huh. Weird.

She shook off the strange feeling as their flight's luggage started to drop onto the belt. When they'd collected everything, they met Lucy at the car rental desk. She waved the key fob in triumph as Cary handed her her wheely bag.

"Sorry my dads couldn't meet us and bring us leis," Lucy said on the walked out to the shuttle that would take them to the car lot. "They really wanted to since it's Cary and Marianne's first trip here. But there's so much they're dealing with with the ceremony and reception and all, I told them not to make the drive."

"I'm glad you didn't put them to any trouble," Cary said. "I'm even more glad they invited us to their renewal." She grinned and pulled in a deep breath, filling herself up with the sunny Hawaii air, the incident beside the luggage carousel pushed to the back of her mind.

Her first real vacation since becoming Portland's magical Protector.

Here, at least, she knew she wouldn't have to work.

THE TRIP ACROSS THE MOUNTAINS PROVED AS BEAUTIFUL AS LUCY HAD claimed. They took the Pali Highway, so she could take them to the top of the Pali lookout, which gave a spectacular view of the lushly green windward side of the island and the crystal blue Pacific Ocean stretching out beyond. Dark lava rock contrasted with thick green, fragrant plant life and all that white sand and blue ocean…

Cary could see why everyone called this paradise.

Traffic coming over the Pali wasn't too bad that time of day, so they made the rest of the drive in good time. Marianne and Cary spent the entire trip waving at their surroundings and ohing and ahing at the beauty. Even the houses and strip mall they passed after dropping into Kailua seemed prettier. Lucy asked what was so pretty about a grocery store and a drug store, but Marianne just insisted it was and not to argue with her about it.

And because Lucy risked a rebellion from Angie if they didn't get food sooner rather than later, she took them to Zippy's before taking them to her dads' house.

"See, it's just an ordinary shopping mall," Lucy said, pointing to the mall next to the parking lot where the restaurant was located.

"Do they have Hawaiian shirts, and surfer gear, and macadamia nut things in that mall?" Marianne asked, hands on her hips.

"Well, yeah, of course," Lucy said. "It's Hawaii."

"My point," Marianne said. As if she'd really made one.

Zippy's food was just as delicious as Lucy had promised. Though Cary refused to even try the spam. She drew the line as canned spiced ham, even if Lucy proclaimed it the best thing ever.

Angie didn't talk much until she'd finished the last few scoops of rice on her plate. Then she leaned back with a satisfied sigh and said, "Now we can go meet your fathers."

The rest of the drive only took about twenty minutes, driving down the Kahekili Highway, past a large cemetery with a Japanese Buddhist Temple nestled against the mountains near the rear of the hilly grounds.

"If we have time, I'll take you there to feed the koi and ring the bell," Lucy said. "Even overrun with tourists, the Byodo-In Temple is one of my favorite spots."

They turned down a road going a little farther up into the hills. The streets were lined with one story wooden houses and the occasional home built up on stilts with the area under the stilts crammed with various beach going equipment—surfboards, bodyboards, sometimes kayaks—as well as bikes and cars and the stuff Cary was used to seeing in people's garages.

Lucy's family home was about halfway up the hill, on a street facing the ocean so that when Cary climbed out of the car, she could just see the blue expanse over the rooftops.

"We get to go to the beach at some point, right?" she asked, dragging her gaze away from that slice of cool blue. The windward side, true to its name, was breezy and not nearly as hot as the leeward side of the island had been, but still pretty warm in late May, and the cold ocean waves beckoned.

"Tomorrow we'll do a whole tourist day," Lucy promised. "Including spending some time on the beach."

"How'd you grow up in all this sun with your skin tone?" Marianne asked cupping her hand over her eyes to shade against the sun before pulling her stylish sunglasses out of a purse that should have been too small to carry the large glasses.

"Where do you think I got all my freckles," Lucy said, rolling her eyes. "We've got lots of sunscreen, don't worry."

"I'm not the one lacking melanin," Marianne said, nodding to Angie and Cary.

"Yes, but Black people can still get sunburns and skin cancer," Lucy said as if she were more the authority on Black skin than Marianne, even though Marianne was Black, and red-headed, freckle-skinned Lucy was most decidedly not. "Especially here in Hawaii. The sun will surprise you, and you'll be burnt before you realize it because the breeze makes you think it's cool."

"I always wear sunscreen," Marianne said, her tone a little testy. "You don't have to lecture me. You don't think I take care of this beautiful skin?"

"Your skin is beautiful which is why I don't want to see it riddled with sunburn and skin cancer," Lucy said back, her little girl's voice heavy with the lecturing tone she got with her students. "Especially not while visiting my home."

A throat clearing from the house broke into the moment, and Lucy turned to face the house with a grin. "Pop!" She dropped her suitcase and threw herself into the arms of the man waiting for her. He lifted her off the ground as if she weighed nothing—which considering she was barely five foot tall, might have been the case for the much larger man she'd just called Pop.

He was probably six foot or so, about Angie's height, thickly muscles through the shoulders and arms, and darkly tanned. His blond hair was sun bleached almost white, and there were laugh lines around his deep blue eyes.

"You made it!" He set Lucy back on her feet. "How was Zippy's?" The man's voice was deep and cheerful and full of enthusiasm, with a flat sort of accent that Cary associated with Californians.

"They loved it." Lucy faced them. "Cary, Angie, Marianne, this is my Pop, Henry Evans. He'll answer to Hank if he's feeling generous. Pop, my friends."

He grinned at them, flashing very white teeth against his tanned skin. "It's a pleasure to meet you all finally. Lucy talks about you all the time."

"Good stuff, I hope," Cary said, only a little leery.

Lucy was the only mundane human of the four of them, though she was a multi-black belt holding, martial arts badass. The rest of them had some kind of tie to the paranormal world. Marianne was a weaver who could do literal magic with cloth, needle, and thread. Angie was a psychic and a witch with spell casting powers Cary could only envy. And Cary…

Well, she'd been a perfectly ordinary, mundane woman too, before Jaxer and her bosses tricked her into her current job. Now, she channeled her bosses Fae magic and acted as a walking, talking Kevlar vest, able to get between good guys and bad guys and keep the good guys safe. She couldn't toss grown men around like they were napkins, the way Lucy could, but she could keep those same men from shooting anyone—which was kind of how she and Lucy had met.

Since becoming friends with Cary, and then Angie and Marianne, Lucy had confronted things she wouldn't have even known existed before. Sometimes, Cary felt a little guilty about that. She'd been tricked into this world but that didn't mean Lucy had to be part of it. Lucy, on the other hand, claimed not to mind because it kept her life interesting.

Interesting was a good word for it.

A second man stepped out of the house, wiping his hands on a kitchen towel. "I'm missing all the introductions," he said with a smile.

"Dad!" Lucy threw herself at her other father. He didn't lift her off the ground, the way Henry had, but he did pull her onto her toes in his hug.

Lucy's Dad was only a little shorter than her Pop, and had shortly cut, straight black hair, dark brown eyes, and a slimmer build than his husband's. He wasn't nearly as tan either. In contrast to Henry's boardshorts and tank top, he wore light tan pants and a muted Hawaiian shirt in purple and white.

"Just came from work?" Lucy asked, patting his chest. "I thought you took the week off?"

"Had to run into the office for an hour for a meeting. Wasn't a big deal."

Henry snorted. To Cary, Angie, and Marianne, he said in a not-so-quiet aside, "He thinks his colleagues will collapse into chaos without his leadership."

This earned him a sigh from his husband. Then to Lucy, "Introduce me before you father gives your friends the wrong impression about me."

"Angie, Marianne, Cary," Lucy said with a wide grin, "this is my dad, Steve Nakada. He works in Honolulu at a banking and investment firm. And the place would descend into chaos without him."

"Ah, thanks, sweetie. I keep telling your father that, but he doesn't believe me."

Henry snorted again, then said with great affection, "Let's get inside before your head grows so much you can't get through the door."

As they hauled luggage into the house, Cary felt another little shiver on her spine. She frowned and glanced around.

It wasn't exactly the feeling she got when there was trouble and her brand of help was needed. And it wasn't the sensation she got when her bosses were about to appear. But it was some flavor of the two. The exact same sensation she'd felt in the airport.

Sort of like she was being watched.

When she studied her surroundings, hunting for the source of the unease, she couldn't pinpoint anything. In fact, the moment she started looking, the sensation ended.

Very weird.

"You okay?" Angie asked, stopping beside her with a large suitcase in tow—the one they'd all used for packing the presents. She scanned their surroundings as well.

"Yeah. I just had a weird feeling, but it was…different to the feelings I usual get." She shook her head. "I'm sure it was nothing."

"Probably just residual jumpiness from work," Angie said. "Everyone gets that the first day or two of vacation. It'll go away."

Cary hadn't considered that. Her first real vacation since taking the job, of course she'd still be jumpy and inclined to see trouble where there was none. It was, as Angie had pointed out, her job.

"You get this way?" she asked as she helped Angie heft the bag into the house.

"Of course. I always spend the first day of a vacation checking the time, thinking I have to meet a client at any moment. I get over it."

Cary glanced back out the door to the sunny residential street, the neat lawns, tropical trees, and flowers perfuming the air. Except for a kid riding by on a bike, all was quiet.

She shook her head. Angie was right. It was probably her imagination. Just a side effect of still being "on" from work. She was sure she'd get over it in a day or two. This was paradise after all.

Nothing to worry about.

2

In the end, it took them two days before they were able to do anything remotely touristy, like go to the beach. Lucy got immediate swept up in last minute details for the wedding and reception, including getting recruited to drive back to Honolulu airport twice over those two days. Once to collect Steve's parents flying in from California for the wedding, and once to pick up Henry's younger brother and mother who arrived from Texas and Arizona respectively, but whose flights arrived close enough together it required only one trip for Lucy.

The chaos was real and fun and a complete distraction. Cary didn't think again about her job, or the weird feelings she'd gotten the day they arrived, or anything else for that matter. She was too busy running errands for Lucy and her fathers to worry. Which was, she had to admit, a nice transition into vacation mindset because by the time they did take a day to do tourist things, she was ready.

At Marianne's urgings, they went to the beach first—a beautiful white sandy beach park, up the coast enough that it wasn't overrun by tourists, but there were a lot of locals taking advantage of the sunshine. Cary only realized it was a Saturday because of all the people.

True to her word, Lucy had a buffet of sunscreens and lotions and after-sun lotions that ensured they were all protected from the tricky sun. Which turned out to be a good thing because Cary still came away from an afternoon spent reading on her towel and swimming in the gloriously cold salt water with a bit of color.

"What would have happened without the lotions," she wondered, looking at her arm.

"Cooked lobster," Lucy said with a knowing nod.

The next day, Lucy took them on a drive up to the North Shore. They had lunch in Haleiwa, the main town on the North part of the island, a cute place full of wooden buildings, shops stuffed with beach gear, and shacks with surfboards stacked up for sale and rent. After a gorgeous lunch of roasted pork, rice, and tropical fruits, Lucy introduced them to a Hawaiian delicacy. Shave ice. The packed, finely grated ice flavored with sweet syrup—in Cary's case a mix of coconut and pineapple because, she reasoned, when you're in Hawaii you should have piña colada flavors—was a delight on the hot afternoon.

Then they shopped for a few hours. Marianne bought two new swimsuits and a sarong. Cary bought some fun surfer t-shirts and the dolphin-covered sarong Marianne talked her into. Angie indulged in some hippy beaded jewelry she said would be good for work.

Near the end of their shopping day, as she waited outside one of the many swimsuit stores they'd visited, though, Cary got that strange sense of being watched again.

She'd just about convinced herself those moments on the day they arrived had been her imagination. Now, she got the distinct impression of…something not quite right. Someone studying her? Definitely someone watching her. And a sense of…

Menace.

But almost as soon as she felt that sense of menace, it vanished.

Whoa. That was weird.

Angie frowned at her when Cary gave a big shiver. Because Cary didn't want anyone to worry, especially Lucy, she said, "Been standing in the shade too long." And stepped out into the sunshine.

The sense of someone watching her didn't return, but she found herself scanning her surroundings more than normal.

The drive back to Lucy's family home took them past some of the most gorgeous scenery Cary had ever seen, passing famous surfing beaches, the world renowned Turtle Bay hotel, and a stretch of protected coast where the clear blue water came up almost to the very edge of the road.

The day after their trip to the North Shore, Lucy insisted they go to the Byodo-In Temple in the Valley of the Temples, the place she'd pointed out to them on their first day. "It's Monday, so there won't be as many tourists as at the weekend. And if we go early, it might even be relatively quiet. It's perfect when there aren't many people there."

The drive was short, so Steve tasked them with picking up some things at the grocery story after their touristing. The renewal ceremony was that Saturday, and everyone was getting more nervous as the big day approached. After watching Lucy's dads organizing the ceremony and reception, Cary was starting to think weddings were maybe more work than they were worth. All that effort and nervousness surrounding something that was supposed to be, in essence, a big party?

Though to be fair, Henry was the frantic one about the details. Steve had decided to step back and let Henry handle everything. Lucy assured them this was the opposite of what normally happened and was apparently leading to some interesting outcomes.

The Temple Valley cemetery was a lovely, hilly place with a guard at an entry gate and a short drive through the rolling hills up to the base of a mountain. Cary climbed out of the car and surveyed the parking lot next to the temple. The day was warm and damp, and the rich scent of tropical plant life and water hung thick in the air. She breathed it in, holding it for as long as she could. A bank of trees blocked the temple from view here. A ticket booth and a bridge at the end of the parking lot led into the sacred area. There were only three other cars in the lot, which meant they wouldn't have to fight for space next to other tourists. At least not yet. The sounds of running water, the breeze through the leaves, and bird song filled the air.

"So beautiful," Marianne murmured.

Lucy handed her a spray can of bug repellant. "Wait till we get inside. But first, this. There's enough still water and we're far enough away from ocean that mosquitos can be a real problem here if you have sweet blood."

"Everything about me is sweet," Marianne said with a little grin as she applied the repellant.

Once they were all sufficiently able to fend off biting bugs, they got their tickets and made their way over the bridge, which spanned a beautifully scenic river running through the middle of thick green foliage, and into the temple grounds proper. The temple itself was a huge, glorious edifice of elegantly arched dark wood with a roof that curved upward at the corners, portions of the outer building painted red and gold, the walls mostly open so that the giant Buddha statue inside the inner sanctum was just visible.

An expansive green pond took up the space in front of the temple. To their left, a huge brass bell hung inside an open-sided structure with a curved roof. A wooden log hung from ropes in front of the bell. To their right, more pond and a small building Lucy said contained nick-knacks for the souvenir-inclined as well as fish food for the koi in the ponds. A huge peacock strolled past, but kept its tail unfortunately down.

"I'd like to ring the bon-sho before we go in," Lucy said, her voice a little hushed now that they were inside the grounds.

She pulled a dollar from her backpack purse and headed toward the bell house. After pushing her folded bill into a little wooden donations box, Lucy hauled back on the rope holding the log, kept the log up in the air for a beat, and then let go. The gong hit the bell with a resounding *bong*, the note echoing through the valley. Lucy caught the rope so the log didn't hit the bell a second time, ensuring it came to stillness before she moved on.

A little bridge crossed over a part of the pond, and a myriad of bright orange koi, to reach the inner sanctum. Before turning onto the bridge, Cary spotted another smaller structure farther up the hill to their left, at the end of a pathway lined in large flat stone steps.

"That's a meditation spot, right next to a waterfall," Lucy said when she noticed the direction of Cary's gaze. "We'll go there before we leave. That's my favorite spot in the grounds."

Taking their shoes off at the entrance, they passed through the inner sanctum of the temple so Lucy could light a stick of incense and say hi to the Buddha statue. It was a huge, gorgeous brass creation that Cary spent a good deal of time admiring as the scent of incense and burning candles filled the already fragrant air. They retrieved their shoes and walked outside the temple to the opposite bridge leading to the souvenir shop where they bought a few trinkets—Cary picked out a lovely Japanese fan—and some fish food to feed the already fat koi. The peacock, with his tail still down, spent a great deal of time watching them as if expecting some food of his own.

"Don't feed the peacocks," warned the lady behind the counter in the shop. "You not careful, they bite."

After ensuring the koi stayed fat, Lucy circled them back to the stone steps so they could see the meditation temple. More people were starting to fill the grounds, though there were still few enough Cary felt like they had some privacy as they walked up to the open-sided temple next to a small, bubbling waterfall.

The structure was a circular, miniature version of the larger temple, with red painted columns holding up a decoratively tiled roof with upswept corners. The sounds of water trickling over rocks and down a small narrow stream blocked out the sounds of people only a short distance away and really gave the area a peaceful vibe. Lucy sat at the pentagonal wooden bench inside the temple and faced the waterfall, dropping into a quiet, meditative stare as the rest of them settled on the bench next to her. Cary had a view of the waterfall and the wall of mountain and trees that butted up against the back of the temple grounds. The mountains on this side of the island were sheer and steep, showing their volcanic origins, now covered by lush forests.

Cary wondered when was the last time she'd felt this sense of peace and quiet. Before becoming a Protector? Earlier than that? There was a stillness here that seeped into her soul and settled her. She understood why this was Lucy's favorite spot now.

And she would have walked away from that spot feeling happy and replenished…

If not for the dragon that walked out of the shallow river.

On first glance, Cary would have assumed the dragon was just a lizard of some kind escaped from a zoo or some irresponsible pet owner. It looked large enough, but nothing unusual for, say, a komodo dragon. Greenish scales. A large, angular head and thick shoulders. Forked tongue flicking out to taste the damp air.

And then it fully emerged from the stream, slithering over the dark soil onto the shore.

No way to fool herself into thinking it was an ordinary giant lizard at that stage.

Her heart thumped hard as more and more of the creature slid from the pool at the base of the waterfall. There was no way that much animal should have been hiding in so little water. The creature was serpentine slender, its head seeming to grow as more of it moved onto the land until there was no mistaking it for anything but a dragon. Now that it was no longer submerged, its scaled hide glistened blue-green, like the ocean, in a beautiful pattern of iridescent colors. Four thick legs tipped with sharp claws, and a tail that seemed just an extension of the long body. Eyes black, fathomless, and impossible to read.

The forked tongue flicked the air again.

And that sense of threat Cary had felt yesterday in Haleiwa hit again as she stared into the creature's eyes.

She barely had time to register that this was real, and that a dragon had just crawled out of the stream, when the creature rose up onto its hind legs, towering over them for a terrifying moment before shrinking back to something closer to human size.

Cary broke free of her surprise, launched to her feet, and placed herself between her friends and the creature just as it started to shimmer. A glow filled the air around it, sparkling and bright enough to make Cary squint, encompassing the dragon so fully she couldn't see it any more. She glanced around frantically. There were people at the base of the stone steps moving in and out of the temple. The sounds of children giggling at the koi. Another bang on the temple bell echoing through the steep mountains.

The glow dimmed, fading away until Cary could look at the dragon again.

And a woman stood before them.

She was beautiful, with long thick black hair, tan skin, and eyes as black as the dragon's had been. A circular crown woven of palm fronds and flowers sat regally on top of her head. Around her neck, she wore a necklace of dark brown beads, similar to the Kukui nut leis Cary had seen in tourist shops, but this one looked more…substantial. She wore a shimmering green and blue cloth wrapped around her to make a dress, covering everything but her arms. Bare toes poked out from beneath the folds of delicate material.

Lucy gasped.

Over her shoulder, without looking away from the woman, Cary said, "Know her?"

Lucy didn't answer.

The woman spoke in a quiet voice that nevertheless seemed to echo through Cary's bones. "You should not be here. Protector."

Cary blinked a few times. "Uhm," she managed.

"Your kind are not allowed here. Your kind are not welcome in our islands."

Oh shit. "Uh," she managed again, because she was actually too shocked to respond with coherence. "I didn't know that."

"She's here as my guest," Lucy said, standing quickly and coming to Cary's side.

But, Cary noted, staying just behind her shoulder, which meant Lucy was protected from the woman, whoever she was. Cary approved of Lucy's precaution. People had to let Cary protect them for her shield to work properly. If Lucy had tried to step around her, Cary's shield wouldn't have been able to keep her safe.

"You brought a Protector to our shores," the woman said to Lucy. "This is forbidden by treaty."

"I didn't know either," Lucy said, sounding choked.

It was the sound of Lucy's fear and panic that pushed Cary out of her shock.

"I'm just here to attend a wedding," Cary said frantically. "Vacation. That's all. Not here as a Protector. Not on the job or anything. Just a vacation." She was babbling, wasn't she? Probably. But facing a shapeshifter dragon—was that what the woman was?—and being told she was in trouble for even being in Hawaii had addled her.

"You have still broken our treaty with the Fae by coming here. We were not warned you would disturb our islands."

"I am really really sorry about that," Cary said, her heart pumping harder. She wanted to offer to leave immediately, but she also didn't want to upset Lucy's fathers so close to their wedding. "I will leave on Sunday," she promised. "Just get through the wedding and I'm out of here. No harm, no foul."

"It is too late for that, Protector," the woman said, and the sound of her voice grew deeper and more menacing. "You must atone." She glanced at Lucy. "You have been given a home in our islands, child. You must atone as well."

"Woah, wait." Cary raised her hands, palms facing the dragon-woman. "Listen, Lucy didn't do anything wrong. Not on purpose. If someone had told me I wasn't allowed here, I wouldn't have come."

And wasn't that something she was going to discuss with the Nags when she got home. Why the hell hadn't they told her Protectors weren't supposed to come to Hawaii? She'd have thought that was a very important bit of information to convey while they were arguing about her taking this vacation.

"The damage has been done. Atonement is the only option."

"Uhm," Cary said again, because she wasn't sure she liked the sound of "atonement."

"The spirits of Hawaii demand your labor, in exchange for our forbearance."

Cary's eyebrows shot up. She glanced at Lucy. Lucy shook her head, still staring wide-eyed at the dragon-woman.

"The huaka'i pō walk tonight."

The woman's voice echoed like a drum, and for a terrifying moment, Cary thought all this would draw the attention of some poor innocent tourist, and then she'd have even more trouble on her hands.

Lucy gasped. "Night marchers."

"Night marchers?" Cary looked between Lucy and the dragon-woman.

"Ghosts," Lucy murmured.

Ghosts? Cary's knees wobbled. She was terrified of ghosts. Scared out of her ever-loving mind of ghosts. She'd seen and faced a lot of things since becoming a Protector. But ghosts… Nope, nope, nope, nope, nope…. She couldn't. She just couldn't.

"In the Kualoa valley," the woman continued, heedless of Cary's terror. "You must go there tonight."

"I, uh, don't you have…something else we could do?" Panic made her voice squeak. She swallowed. Tried again. "Some other way for us to atone. That doesn't involve…ghosts." Her heart hammered so hard, she was afraid she'd hyperventilate. She focused on slowing her breathing.

"This is what you must do," the woman said. "You must go to the valley, you must stop those who would interfere with the marchers."

"Wait," Lucy said, "someone is dumb enough to try interfering with the night marchers?"

Cary wanted to ask questions but was too busy trying not to pass out. Ghosts? Not ghosts. Anything but ghosts.

"Those who are trying to…use them, they must be stopped. You two will stop them."

"And there's no one else you can send to do this?" Cary asked, barely managing to get her voice above a whisper. Shit, that didn't sound very brave, did it? "I mean, I'm not supposed to be here, I get that. And I'm really really sorry. But, shouldn't this be something handled by, I don't know, Hawaiians?"

"You will go to the valley," the woman said as if Cary hadn't spoken. "You will do what you must. This is your charge. Your quest. Do this, or you will not be forgiven for bringing uninvited magic to our shores. Our anger demands a steep price."

Since this was Lucy's home, and she *had* to be able to return, Cary wanted to ensure Lucy wasn't banned or anything. But…

Ghosts.

"No other options?" she asked. "Ghosts are the only way we can make sure Lucy's forgiven for a mistake she didn't know she was committing?"

"There is no other option, Protector. You two must atone. You will defend the night marchers. Ensure no one else is killed. Then you will be forgiven."

"Wait, 'no one else' implies someone has been killed," Cary said. "Who's been killed?"

The woman shifted her black-eyed gaze to Lucy, ignoring Cary's question. "You are a warrior. Tonight you will be their warrior. You will save them."

"Me?" Lucy's already high voice went another octave higher. Cary heard her gulping swallow clearly. "I… How can I save ghosts?"

Cary shivered again, hard.

"You will do this," the dragon-woman said to Lucy. "You are being called by the spirits of your adopted home."

"I thought we were apologizing for an accident?" Cary said. Then clamped her mouth shut as the dragon-woman turned her gaze back to Cary's and the sense of menace washed over her again. There was nothing in that gaze Cary could read, though. Nothing to appeal to. Just black black eyes and an impenetrable stare.

"You have been called by the spirts of the islands to undertake this quest. You can only earn our forgiveness if you complete this task."

Cary might have thought to ask what happened if they *weren't* forgiven, if they declined the quest and just took the displeasure of the spirits of the islands on the chin. Except that she couldn't do that to Lucy. This was Lucy's home. Lucy's family was here. Cary couldn't risk endangering her place here, even if they'd done that on accident.

"We've got your backs," Angie murmured. "Don't worry. We'll do this together."

The black-eyed woman turned her head a little. "Witch. Weaver." The words were spoken like a greeting.

"She knows a lot about us," Marianne murmured. "I'm not exactly wearing a sign."

"Yup," Angie said.

The woman's gaze turned back to Lucy. "You must answer this call. Fight for the ancient warriors."

"Fight what?" Cary said. "Who? And for what reason? You haven't explained…anything." Especially how *ghosts* could be in danger. Anything that threatened ghosts had to be very very bad, right?

"Go to the Kualoa valley. Into the hills. Tonight. Fulfill this quest. Or suffer our anger."

"No," Lucy and Cary said at the same time. "Wait," Cary added.

But the woman shimmered again, the glow rising around her. Cary narrowed her eyes against the glare. When the light faded, the dragon was back. Its long, forked tongue flickered out at them once, and then it turned and slipped back into the stream.

Disappearing into waters not nearly deep enough to hold it.

4

The silence filling the meditation area felt a lot heavier and a lot less peaceful in the wake of the dragon-woman's disappearance.

And yet, water still bubbled over rocks. A gentle breeze filtered through the trees and ferns. Sun dappled the ground near the stream. The scents of damp forest and flowers perfumed the air. In the distance, people still laughed at the koi.

All as if nothing had just happened.

"Well that was…" Lucy started.

"Yeah," Cary said. "But what do we—"

"We shouldn't go into the mountains at night," Lucy said.

"I agree," Cary said, "but…"

Lucy sucked her lips into her mouth, blinking hard at the spot the woman had been. "But how do I say no to one of the Hawaiian goddesses?" she said quietly after a moment.

"A goddess?"

"Or a spirit," Lucy said, shrugging. "Depends on your definitions. She's not one of the major gods, but there are a lot of them here. Or… Well, I didn't consider them to be *real* entities. Just stories. Part of Hawaiian traditions and legends."

"Old gods," Angie said. Cary and Lucy faced her. "Gods of different lands, part of the land itself, often elemental parts of nature."

"Like Pele is the goddess of fire and volcanos," Lucy said, "And Kane is the god of all living things."

"Old gods don't stir themselves often these days," Angie said. "At least not in my experience."

"So we were *really* talking to a god?" Cary said.

"Depends on your perspective," Lucy said again. "If it's easier, you can think of her as a nature spirit."

"Not any easier," Cary said. Spirits were a little too shoulder-to-shoulder with ghosts. "Now what?"

"We have to go to Kualoa tonight," Lucy said.

"You just said we shouldn't," Cary pointed out.

"Shouldn't isn't the same as won't," she said reasonably. But the freckles across her nose stood out sharper now against her pale skin, belying the matter-of-factness she was attempting. "A Hawaiian spirit has…asked me to do this. I can't refuse her."

Ask was not the word Cary would have used. Ordered. Demanded. Threatened.

But technically, the word didn't matter, did it. They had to do this to ensure Lucy was safe here going forward. Not doing it was a risk too great to take with Lucy's home and family.

Cary blew out a loud breath. "We don't even know what we're supposed to do there. We're…protecting the ghosts? Did I get that part right?"

"Got me," Lucy said. "The whole thing is more than a little unusual."

"You sure you want to do this?" Angie asked, her gaze on the stream.

"You think something's wrong?" Lucy asked.

As the resident witch, and someone who'd done… Well, Cary wasn't exactly sure *what* Angie had done in the past, but she definitely had enough experience in this whole paranormal world that Cary trusted her opinions.

"Not sure," Angie said. "Getting a weird feeling. The aura on the spirit-goddess was…interesting. Bright as you might expected."

"Sure sure," Cary said, as someone who couldn't read auras and had no idea what Angie meant through direct experience.

"But…swirly? That's not right." She sighed. "Not sure how to explain it." She shrugged. "Nature spirits are hard to read. Just… Plenty left unsaid."

"Well that's true," Lucy said with a scowl. "But one way or the other, I'd better do this." She looked at Cary. "You okay with this? I know it's ghosts…" Lucy winced. They all knew how Cary felt about ghosts.

But Cary didn't even hesitate. "I'm your shield tonight. You can count on that. I can't do much else, especially about ghosts, but I can keep the rest of you safe from here to eternity."

Lucy's smile bloomed. "Thanks." She glanced at Marianne and Angie again. "I know you said you'd help, but…"

"Don't even start," Marianne said.

"We'll be there," Angie said.

"You walked into a goblin horde with me," Marianne said. "We can face some ghosts with you."

Cary squeezed her eyes shut as they group hugged, working very hard not to shudder.

Ghosts.

5

———————

The grounds behind the Kualoa Ranch house and parking lot, where they'd parked the car, were pitch black, with only a sliver of moon to provide light. Mountains rose above them in dark, hulky shadows waiting to descend like crashing waves. The damp grass underfoot squelched as they moved across the low hills at the base of the mountain. Night in Hawaii smelled a lot like day in Hawaii, the air rich with tropical plants and salt water, but Cary was sure she wasn't imagining the faintly sweet scent of rotting detritus under the more luscious tropical scents.

Or maybe she was. She'd been imaging a lot since they moved into these foothills. She was shivering so hard her flashlight beam kept bouncing around. And she'd had to suppress more than one squeak or startled jump when the beam caught movement. Movement that was mostly their own shadows or moving grass.

"How far into the mountains do we have to go?" she murmured, her ears hurting as she strained to hear any hint of danger. So far, all she heard was the rustle of grass in the wind, which was stronger tonight than it had been during the day, and an occasional night bug or bird.

"There aren't any rats out here, are there?" Marianne asked, her flashlight sweeping in a wide arc across the grass. On the second day in Hawaii, Lucy had told them about the rat problem farther up on the mountain in her neighborhood, and Marianne had been freaked out about those and the flying cockroaches ever since.

Cary could relate. She wasn't big on rats either even though she'd had to dissect one in college. But she'd had to help with treatment on someone's pet rat when she'd still been a vet tech, and that had calmed a lot of her anti-rat sentiments. Gregory had been a lovely little boy. At the moment, however, she was so much more worried about ghosts that rats and cockroaches ranked very low on her worry list.

"I'm sure they'll steer clear of the area," Lucy said, her voice quiet, "since the marchers are out tonight."

"Stop," Cary begged. "I'm wigged out enough as is."

"I still can't believe you're afraid of ghosts," Lucy said, sounding faintly amused. "You face down demons and shapeshifters and assholes all the time."

"Not *all* the time," she muttered. "Sometimes they're vampires."

"Aren't they essentially dead people, too?" Lucy asked.

"But they aren't ghosts. They're solid. I can poke them in the eye if I have to."

Lucy paused, long enough Cary thought she might be laughing at her. Then Lucy said, "You actually have a point."

Finally! Someone agreed with her. Lucy, of all of them, being the one most able to use physical force should be the one most understanding of Cary's fear.

"Holy hell," Lucy muttered and stopped moving forward.

Cary froze, sure she'd seen the ghosts. Or at least seen the light about being terrified of ghosts. Then the muttered sounds of voices seeped in past the sound of her own pounding heartbeat.

She hurriedly put herself between Lucy and the voices. They were distant, but in the darkened hills, sound carried strangely so she wasn't sure how far away the people possessing those voices actually were.

Lucy came up close to her but stayed firmly behind her. Marianne and Angie clumped up at her back, too. All of them, without speaking, turned their flashlights off.

Darkness dropped over them like a blanket, filling the area so thoroughly that for a long moment Cary couldn't see anything at all. She waited for her night vision to adjust, knowing if anything dangerous was out there, they were safe because her magic kicked in when she was between good guys and bad guys and the people at her back were definitely the good guys. If anything in front of them—or even behind them for that matter because you couldn't get around Protector powers just by sneaking up on people—was a danger, Cary's magic would automatically raise the shields.

Her confidence wavered, though, when a new worry poked its head out of the stygian darkness. She drew her magic from her bosses' magic. She channeled what they gave her. But they were North American Fae, and she hadn't asked if their magic extended to Hawaii. Given the fact that she wasn't supposed to be here, that the dragon-woman had told her she'd broken treaties being here, would she even be able to channel Protector magic?

She'd been fine in New York—and to be fair had only had to do a little Protecting while visiting her sister; couple of almost muggings and one near car accident, nothing too obvious or taxing; though the car accident had been interesting to explain—but that was still North American. There were Protectors scattered all over North America, according to Jaxer. The magic worked anywhere in the region.

But it hadn't occurred to her to ask if her ability to channel magic extended beyond the boundaries of North America.

Oops.

She swallowed hard as that worry settled in. But the dragon-woman wouldn't have charged her to do this quest if her magic wasn't working here, right? She'd specifically said Cary had brought foreign magic into the islands. And that's why she had to be out here with ghosts. Her powers surely worked here.

Right?

Over her shoulder to Angie, she whispered, "Maybe you should set a circle around us. Just in case."

"You worried about the ghosts still? Cause my circle can keep out ghosts."

"That is amazing to hear. And yes, still worried about ghosts." But also about her own shield.

"We won't be able to stop whatever's a threat to the marchers if we stay inside a witch protective circle, though," Angie said, her deep voice quiet and remarkably soothing in the darkness.

Cary's vision was just starting to adapt, so that now she could make out the looming darker shapes of mountains ahead of them. That helped lessen her worry and panic a little, too.

"We'll have to leave the circle at some point," Lucy said, "despite the ghosts, if we're going to save the ghosts."

"Which is still a really strange quest," Marianne pointed out.

Cary agreed wholeheartedly.

"But maybe the protective circle would be good before we have to do that," Cary said, trying not to squeak. She didn't want to admit she was worried about her shield working and risk worrying her friends. But it was hard to keep her voice both quiet and steady. Keeping quiet seemed important, though. She had no idea how far sound carried in these hills, and she didn't want to give them away to whoever was still out there.

The voices from ahead got louder suddenly, as if to confirm her suspicion that sound would do weird things here, and finally she heard movement through the grass. Though the voices were hushed, they grew clearer. She could pick out a direction. In front and to the right of them. Between the wind and the general quiet, she only caught snatches of their conversation, not enough to make out any words or even judge who the people might be, but enough she knew they were a lot closer now.

And getting closer fast.

There wasn't enough time for Angie to build a protective circle before the approaching people reached them.

Which meant Cary was about to find out the hard way if her magic worked or not.

6

The approaching group of people sounded small enough, maybe three or four of them. Which put Cary and her friends on even footing with whoever was out there. She had to hope that was good for her side. Especially if something went wrong with her shield.

Wind churned the air, swirling the scents of tropical forest with the faint hint of salty sea air around her face. Between the wind and the pitch darkness, she was almost cold. She had on jeans—because she wasn't sure what to expect here—and a loose sweatshirt she hadn't thought she'd need to wear. Still she shivered as the voices neared.

Just from the cold breeze, she was sure.

The people approaching didn't have flashlights on either, at least not that Cary could pick out. She was sure she'd have seen any source of light they carried with them by now, given how dark it was. But thanks to her night vision having kicked in, she could see the shapes of three…no, four people topping a hill a few hundred yards away.

Realizing she could see them, better than she normally would have been able to, made her wobble with relief. She let out a long, low sigh.

"Powers working?" Angie murmured in her ear so the others wouldn't hear.

Of course Angie had realized Cary was worried about that. The fact that Angie hadn't been certain Cary's powers would work either, though, wasn't reassuring. She nodded to answer Angie's question and angled a little so she was more firmly between her friends and the strangers.

It occurred to her that these could just be people out hiking in the dark for the thrill of it. Or Ranch staff. They didn't necessarily have to be up to something nefarious. They might not be the people who were a threat to the marchers.

But Cary wasn't taking any chances. Especially since her powers *were* working, which meant there was danger around here somewhere.

As the four people neared, she was finally able to hear their conversation.

"This isn't working," a distinctly deep male voice said.

"We've tried four times," another said. "This is stupid."

"The witch said this would work," a third, more feminine voice said. "It will work."

"It's taking too long," the first voice said. "We're gonna get caught. You heard the news report. That last guy died."

"In a car accident," the woman said. "Nothing to do with us."

"We shouldn't be messing with this," the second man said.

"Without the marchers, what do we have? Some creepy nighttime footage. That's not what we're getting paid for," the woman hissed. "We need *this*. We'll never get network attention without it. That's the job."

"And there a lot of money on the line," a fourth person said. The fourth's voice was quiet and intense.

"This is going bad," the first voice said.

"We shouldn't be messing in this supernatural stuff," the second man said.

"You keep saying that," the woman said, "but you're still here, aren't you?"

"I want this, too. But locals have died."

"Accidents."

"You know the marchers been looking at them. And that's our fault."

"That wasn't the plan," the first man said.

"Yeah, no one's supposed to die," the second man said.

"You really think that?" the woman asked, sounding incredulous.

During all this, the four people were walking straight toward Cary and her group without seeming to notice them. Maybe their night vision wasn't as good as Cary's was in that moment. She wanted to ask if any of her friends could see the strangers. They all seemed to be ordinary humans, at least that's what the conversation led her to believe. If Lucy couldn't see very well still, it meant the four approaching probably couldn't see Cary's group.

Would the element of surprise be a good thing in this case or not so much?

"Put the fucking gun away," the woman hissed over her shoulder to one of the other shadows. "That won't help against ghosts. Idiot."

So. Surprise and a gun probably wouldn't be a good combination. Cary cleared her throat.

All four people stopped in their tracks.

"Who's there?" the first man said, gesturing in their direction.

"Just concerned citizens," Cary said. "But, uh..." What did she say? We're here to stop you from doing something with the ghosts that's apparently getting people killed, but we have no real idea what you're doing? That seemed...easy to misinterpret.

"You're trespassing," the woman said.

Cary could see her straightening her shoulders and pulling herself into a more upright posture, but Cary still couldn't make out anyone's features clearly. The voices and physical shapes of the four people seemed to indicate three men and a woman, but she couldn't be certain.

"So are you," Lucy answered. "And trying to harm the marchers."

"They ghosts," the second voice said, moving up closer to the woman. "What you know anyway, sistah?"

"I know the river spirit who sent us here told us you were a threat and were getting people killed," Lucy said.

"No idea what you're talking about. How old you, anyway, six?"

"Fuck you," Lucy said cheerfully. "And for that crack, I'll kick your ass first."

The man snorted. "Right. We're really afraid of you."

"I wouldn't underestimate her," Cary said. "But beyond that, those deaths were apparently not accidents but something to do with what you're doing here with the marchers." At least that's what she had to assume, given the vague hints the dragon-woman had given them and the worry the group had expressed themselves.

"How you know anything?" the second man said.

Well, he was chatty. He also wasn't the one holding a gun, at least not that Cary could make out. He did have full hands, with equipment that, after staring hard for a moment, Cary realized was a very large camera and a tripod.

The first man who'd spoken also had his hands full with some boxes. And the woman had a backpack on her shoulder.

The fourth person held the gun, pointed in their direction. The gun barrel was a steady black shadow, no wobbling or hesitance.

Cary swallowed. She hated getting shot. But since she wasn't throwing herself in front of the bullet, it would have time to stop and she probably wouldn't get hurt. Probably.

All things considered, though, she preferred getting shot at than ghosts, so that was at least one upside.

"What *are* you all doing here anyway?" Cary asked. "All the camera equipment and boxes? You, like, a film crew? Amateurs if you're looking for a network spot, am I right? Is this some ghost hunters attempt or something? You mentioned a witch. What was all that about?"

She'd discovered, since becoming a Protector, that her superpower —besides freezing in place so bad guys couldn't get at good guys— was an ability to irritate people into telling her things. It didn't always work. But it was a nice distraction even when they refused to divulge their nefarious plans.

The woman's turn to sniff in distain. "You think this is some silly fake documentary we're filming? No."

"Oh, do explain," Cary said, yawning loudly and obviously as if bored, because, well…pushing buttons. She was kind of hoping they could end this before the ghosts showed up.

"Should I shoot her?" the man with the gun asked.

Cary grinned, and wondered if they could see it in the dark. "Go ahead," she said. "How many bullets do you have in that thing? Go ahead and empty it. I dare you."

She really preferred when the guns were empty. Empty guns were a lot less dangerous. Still a chunk of hard metal if they hit you, but no more flying projectiles was always good.

"You hate getting shot," Lucy reminded her, in a not so quiet voice.

"I know. But whatever. I'm on vacation. I'll have time to heal."

The woman glanced sideways at her companions. "You get shot a lot?" she asked.

Cary waved a hand in the air. "It happens. You know. Day in the life, right?"

"You crazy?" the second man asked, taking a step back.

"You're out here hunting ghosts and you're asking if *I'm* crazy?" Cary shook her head at him. "I'd rethink my definitions of that word if I were you."

"We don't have time for you," the woman said after a moment. "Get out of the way or I'll let my friend here shoot you."

Cary shrugged. "Well, I'm not going anywhere. I do what river spirits tell me to do when they show up in person in the shape of a dragon and are mad at me."

"What the fuck you talking about?" the second man spat.

"The river spirit. From the stream. The one who told us to stop you. The old god. That one."

The first man took a step behind the woman and murmured something close to her ear. Cary's hearing got better when she was in full Protector mode, but nothing like, say, a shifter's hearing, so she had no idea what they said to each other. She did notice the fourth man adjusting his stance a little. The gun in his hand wasn't wobbling, even a little bit, which was…well, kind of intimidating if she were honest with herself. How the hell could he hold a gun up like that without getting tired? Did he have a lot of practice holding guns on people for long periods of time? That was a scary thought.

"Listen," the woman said, her tone changing to something conciliatory. "You're right, we're just a film crew looking to get some ghost footage. No big deal. I can't imagine why anyone would be worried about us. No reason for this to turn into a thing. We can all just go our separate ways."

"No," Lucy said. "And obviously, we don't buy that or you wouldn't need a gun."

"Plus," Cary said, "you just said you weren't out here to film some, and I quote, 'silly fake documentary.' So why are you out here with all that camera equipment?"

"Your other two friends talk?" the first man said.

"Of course," Angie said.

"When necessary," Marianne added.

Then neither said any more. They were practiced in this irritating bad guys stuff too.

Cary smiled at the first man who was still close enough to speak to the woman, his attention was on Cary now. Her vision had cleared more, so she could see the four better. Enough for her to see the first man was pale, his hair on the light side, and he was a little taller than the woman. He was dressed in shorts and a sweatshirt with some sort of logo on it, but she couldn't pick out the logo in the dark.

The woman was probably about Cary height, tallish without being as tall as, say, Angie, and her hair was very dark, tied into a thick braid against skin that was pale but darker than the first man's. Eye color was impossible to tell in the non-existent light, but her eyes seemed dark in her round face. She wore long, pale-colored cargo pants and a fitted, pullover hoodie, which Cary thought looked really comfortable for nighttime in Hawaii.

The second man who'd gotten chatty a moment ago was wide and shortish, what her mother would call stocky, with hair as dark as the woman's pulled into a low tail. He seemed to have tattoos the full length of both arms, but in the dark, Cary couldn't be sure if that was ink or just a second shirt under his tank top.

And how the hell he could wear a tank top, she had no idea. The breeze had kicked up again, and it was getting even cooler on this open hilltop.

The fourth man, with the gun, hung behind the others, and seemed to be more wrapped up in the shadows than the others. Cary could tell he was tallish, around the same height as the first man. A baseball cap covered his hair and cast shadows across his face so even the gleam of his eyes was impossible to see. He was almost as wide as the second man, and wore a windbreaker jacket and long pants.

Outside of the gun, he was the only one not carrying any additional equipment or packs.

Another cold wind brushed across the hill, making Cary shiver. The second man glanced around, moving a little closer to the others. Cary frowned at that.

"I'm really curious what they're up to," she said to Lucy. "This whole thing is weird."

"I agree," she said. "Care to explain?" she asked the strangers.

"No," the woman said.

Cary sighed. "Shame. I prefer a little bad guy monologuing."

"Who says we're the bad guys?" the man with the gun said.

"Your gun and your offer to shoot us earlier," Cary said without looking at him. She was watching the woman.

She'd started to fidget a little and was looking around, her head swiveling as she scanned their surroundings. "Fuck," she muttered.

"Okay," Cary said, "I'm weirded out enough with the whole ghost thing. What's got you all spooked now?"

"Don't like ghosts," the second man said, but he was also watching their surroundings.

"Do you?" Cary asked, in all seriousness. "Especially ones that seem to be responsible for people dying."

"Coincidences," the woman said.

"I don't believe in those," Cary said.

"They happen," the man with the gun said.

"Right," Lucy answered. "Which was why the river spirit sent us here."

"Not sure what you've been smoking, sistah," the second man said, "but I take some of it."

"Something's stirring," Angie murmured.

"Can you…see anything?" Cary asked.

"Ghosts aren't my bag," Angie said. "Need a medium for that kind of *seeing*."

Cary shivered. She couldn't imagine anything as horrifying as being a medium. But that was probably because…well, ghosts were terrifying. As terrifying as clowns. Even more terrifying.

"I can feel something approaching, though," Angie finished.

Cary's heartbeat kicked up with all the worry she could practically feel seeping off the strangers. This wasn't good. But what the hell were they supposed to do?

"What are we supposed to do?" she murmured to Lucy.

"Got me," Lucy said. "I'm not a medium either. Or a witch. Or a… anything else. I'm not sure what the hell we're doing here."

"River spirit dragon-woman. We have to do what she said. Remember." Cary wasn't sure why she was reminding Lucy of this. She was scared and was having a hard time with ordinary things like logic.

Did Protector magic work against ghosts? She had no idea. She tried to avoid ghosts and anything to do with them. She even avoided the bookshelf on ghosts at the Bookstore. So far in her Protector career, she'd been able to avoid everything to do with ghosts. She was more than a little terrified this would be the moment her magic didn't work against the one thing she was most scared of.

"We have to set up," the woman hissed at the men. "If we don't we'll lose our chance."

"Set what up?" Cary asked, her gaze darting around the dark hills.

Lucy leaned in very close to Cary. "Whatever happens, whatever marches out of the mountains, don't look at them. That's how you get dead. Look at them and you or someone you love ends up dead. That's the legend."

She'd kept her voice quiet, for Cary, Marianne, and Angie, but

Cary saw the second man's gaze jump to them before he went back to scanning his surroundings.

"Set up," the woman hissed.

The two men carrying equipment dropped their various armfuls of stuff. Second Man started putting together what Cary had assumed was a camera and tripod. It still looked like a camera after he had it up, but the front seemed strange looking to her, like the lens was shaped wrong. Very long and narrow, almost like a telescope rather than a camera lens. He steadied the large thing on top of the tripod, flicking closed brackets that snapped as they sealed the camera down in place.

The First Man opened up a few of the dropped boxes and started taking things out that looked like…

"Are they making an altar?" she whispered to Angie.

"They did mention a witch earlier," Angie said.

"I'd assumed that was lighting stuff and maybe infrared for nighttime filming," Marianne said.

"This isn't good, is it?" Lucy murmured.

"Nope," Angie said.

"Got any idea what they're setting up?" Cary asked Angie.

"Nope," she said again.

That wasn't helpful. But powerful as Angie was, she couldn't know everything. And since this had to do with ghosts and she wasn't a medium…

Cary shuddered again and faced the woman. "What *are* you doing? It's going to bug me if I can't figure it out."

"Tough," the woman said.

"I hate when they don't monologue," Cary muttered. It was so much easier when the bad guys just divulged their nefarious plans.

Maybe she'd been working on the wrong bad guy. Chatty Second Man might be a better wedge. Or maybe Gun Man, although he seemed content to just stand there holding a gun on them. Very steadily. Without a single tremor. Wasn't he getting tired?

The First Man seemed to be more restrained and intent, like the woman, so Cary didn't think he'd provide much information. He alternated between glancing around and setting up what was now clearly an altar of some kind. Using the boxes like a table, he set out a layer of palm fronds, then on top placed a few lava rocks, a half clam shell, a conch, and around the setup, a fresh flower lei. He pulled out a water bottle and poured some water into the clam shell, then sprinkled something that was either beach sand or salt—too hard to tell in the dark—over the water.

While he worked, he murmured under his breath. Cary couldn't hear him clearly but the words didn't sound English. She couldn't tell if they were Hawaiian though, or some other language she didn't speak —which included all other languages besides English because she sucked at languages even though she'd been trying to learn some for moments like this when she was trying to decipher spells.

"Got any more clues?" Cary asked Angie. "Or you?" this to Lucy.

"Pretty standard looking altar set up for a witch," Angie said. "Not seeing anything specific enough to give me a hint."

"Got me," Lucy said. "Outside of hearing the legend told around campfires growing up when we went camping on the Big Island, I didn't know the night marchers were even real."

"Are they…" Cary was guessing here, but this seemed possible given what the dragon-woman had said and everything they were witnessing. "Could they be trying to…capture a ghost? Like, trap one?"

"Like *Ghostbusters*?" Lucy asked.

The man with the gun, who'd kept his attention on them the whole time while his associates set up, twitched a little, the gun tip wavering just a moment before stilling. That was the most Cary had seen him move since first pointing the gun at them. A pretty big tell. They were on to something.

"Maybe not just containment," she murmured. "Maybe for… something more. To use them?"

"What the hell you gonna use a ghost for?" Marianne asked.

"Especially one whose gaze will kill…" Lucy trailed off.

Cary straightened her shoulders. "A weapon?"

"What's that have to do with getting network attention?" Angie murmured, her voice so low now, Cary was pretty sure the others wouldn't hear her over the wind.

Which had kicked up stronger again. Blowing so hard now some of the palm trees on the next hill were bending hard sideways.

"I assumed that had to do with the camera equipment, making a movie or…" Cary shrugged. "No idea. But we made Gun Man twitch when we mentioned *Ghostbusters*. We're on to something with the trapping idea."

"Can a witch make a spell to trap a ghost?" Lucy asked Angie.

"Sure," Angie said. "With the right training and some element of a medium's magic."

"Mediums have magic?" Marianne asked. "I thought they just talked to ghosts."

"Depends on the medium," Angie said. "Some just talk to ghosts and channel them. Some have more."

All this talk of ghosts had ratchetted Cary's fear up so high she was getting dizzy with it. Her palms were sweating, despite the air seeming to get colder by the moment, her muscles were tense, her gut churning, and she couldn't seem to breathe normally.

She tried to swallow. Tried to calm her pulse. She pulled in a few deep, slow breaths, letting them out as slowly as she'd pulled them in. Concentrating on the fact that she could see pretty well now. Her powers were working.

Seeing the puffs of cold fog on the air as she breathed out didn't entirely help. It shouldn't be cold enough in Hawaii to see your breath. Especially this time of year.

But still. The steady breathing, knowing her powers were working…

Her efforts to calm down could have worked.

Until the drums started.

7

The sounds of drums, distant but clear, traveled like an echo over the hills, bouncing around off the mountains and through the trees. The grass beneath them bent flat in the now fast moving wind. Cary's heartrate, already pounding too hard and fast, tripled.

The bellow of a conch shell trumpeted ahead of the drums.

"What's that?" she muttered, barely able to speak over the fear.

"The night marchers," Lucy said, her high voice so high now she sounded choked.

"Shit," Marianne said.

"Yup," Angie said.

"Hurry," the woman said. "Get that set up in place." She dropped her backpack onto the ground and started pulling things out of it. A bottle of green liquid. Some more palm fronds. A package wrapped to look like a fish, and some fruits. All of this went onto the altar. Except the bottle of green liquid. That, she poured into something at the top of the thing Cary had assumed was a camera.

"I don't like this," Lucy murmured.

Cary nodded. "Me neither." For many many reasons.

The drumbeat drew closer.

"Pretty sure you're right," Angie said, leaning close enough to Cary and Lucy to whisper, "About them trying to capture a ghost. And the camera is the containment vessel."

Cary tried not to shiver again. The air was really cold now, but she couldn't even pretend she was shivering from cold.

"So if they capture a ghost in that camera thingy…" Marianne started.

"And they point the camera thingy at…others," Angie said.

"Which could have others looking at the ghost without meaning to," Lucy said, on a breath.

"Then whoever looked into the camera would die," Cary finished.

"That's some weird ass *The Ring* shit right there," Marianne said.

"I've never seen that movie," Cary said.

"Me neither," Marianne said. "Don't like horror films. The ads were enough."

She'd have fist bumped with Marianne—she didn't like horror movies either—if she weren't so terrified her mind couldn't remember how to make a fist. The hairs on her arms were standing up. And the sound of approaching drums was louder. A low level of mist clung to the damp ground on the hill, starting to obscure the grass. The wind blew so hard the trees were bending over, but it didn't seem to reach the mist which swirled around their feet in gentle eddies.

"I'm thinking more *Poltergeist* and the tv," Lucy said, "but either way, we need to stop this. Poor ghosts."

Poor ghosts? Cary nearly squeaked the question aloud, but couldn't find enough spit to manage words.

"Poor whoever they aim that camera at if they catch a ghost," Angie said.

"They mentioned network attention," Lucy said. "That camera, with a night marcher in it, facing an audience over one of the national network stations, that could lead to a lot of deaths."

"Mass murder?" Cary forced the words out. "But why?"

"Shut up," the man with the gun said.

He'd moved closer while Cary was busy scanning their surroundings, looking for the first hint of approaching ghosts so she'd be sure not to accidentally look at one. She realized her Protector shield would probably keep them safe from deadly night marcher vision, but since she wasn't absolutely positive about that, she didn't want to take any chances.

Having Gun Man get to within a few feet of them without her noticing was a little disconcerting. But at least she *knew* they were safe from him and his gun.

"No one's gonna die," the second, chatty man said. "We not being paid for that."

"Shut up," Gun Man snarled at the Chatty Man. "Or do you really want to tell them everything?"

"If you do, I'll listen," Cary said. "I like when people tell me things."

Gun Man scowled at her.

She shrugged. "I like to learn."

The exchange helped ease her tight gut just enough to allow her some breathing space. The panic slowed to something manageable. But how did they stop the group from doing...whatever it was they were doing without someone getting shot?

Or glared at by a ghost.

Whatever they were going to do, they needed to work fast. The green liquid the woman had poured into the camera had triggered some kind of reaction. A green line ran all around the camera's boxy shape now, twisting over it like a decorative accent, or a space alien suit. The shapes on the sides of the camera formed by the green lines started to move, reforming and forming in a kind of pattern. Words maybe? Hard to tell. If the green lines were making words, those words were disappearing as soon as they formed, giving Cary no time to decipher them.

"What happens if we just knock over the camera and altar?" Cary asked Angie as quietly as possible.

"Depends on what that green liquid was they put into the camera," Angie said. "Even on the ground, it might still have the power to suck in a ghost."

"They've failed at this before," Lucy reminded them. "Others have been up here and stopped them. Outside of the others getting dead, it proves this can be stopped. We can do this."

"Be nice to know if the people who stopped them the previous times used magic or not," Angie said.

"Why?" Cary asked, eyeing Gun Man from her peripheral vision. He was looking back and forth between her group and the group setting up the altar and camera. But he kept the gun solidly trained on Cary and her group.

"If they attempted to stop this with magic," Angie said, "we know that's not a long-term solution. It stopped the group capturing a ghost in the moment but didn't prevent them from trying again."

"If we needed magic, why didn't the dragon-woman tap you more directly?" Marianne asked Angie. "You're the witch. Why didn't she bring you into the conversation when she was accusing Cary and Lucy of needing to atone?"

"Got me," Angie said.

"Maybe magic isn't the answer here," Marianne said. "The dragon-woman didn't say we needed magic."

"Can you move close to the camera?" Lucy asked, sounding contemplative.

Cary frowned down at her. "Probably. What are you thinking?"

"I'm thinking we need to destroy the camera."

"Shouldn't the dragon-woman have told us to bring a hammer, then?" Marianne asked.

"I'm the hammer," Lucy said.

"Huh?" Cary asked.

Lucy gave Cary a look. "You know I break bricks with my bare hands, right? It's part of some of the exhibitions I do."

"I did not know that, actually," Cary said. "I just thought you tossed multiple opponents around to show off your skills at those exhibitions."

"That too," Lucy said with a shrug. "But I can break bricks as well."

"A box full of electronics and magical potion isn't a brick," Angie pointed out. "And for the record, I doubt a simple hammer would work either."

"Why?" Cary asked.

"Someone before us would have tried that already," Angie said.

"Unless they have more than one camera," Marianne said.

"That would be…bad," Cary agreed. "It would help if they'd just tell us their nefarious plan." It was a real pain in the ass when they didn't monologue.

"Move me closer to the camera," Lucy said. "We'll figure it out once we're there."

"I will shoot you if you move," Gun Man said.

"Go for it," Cary said. "Try to avoid the rebound. Be a bitch to explain how you managed to shoot yourself while aiming at someone else."

She started walking toward the camera, her steps careful because even if she could see better now, her companions couldn't and the ground was uneven and impossible to see under the swirling mist.

"You're pretty cocky about getting shot," the woman said, her focus still on the camera and the green lines swirling around it.

"Yup," Cary said. "Happens…well, more than I'd like. I hate guns. Why does everyone have a gun?"

"To keep people from interfering," Gun Man said.

She heard the distinctive metallic click. She didn't know much about guns—outside of occasionally getting shot at, she didn't make an effort to learn about them—but she had the feeling the click was something he did in warning, not something that was necessary. She ignored the warning and moved closer to the camera.

Though she did stretch her hands back to keep her friends safely behind her and within her protection. Even if the Gun Man only wanted to shoot her, shooting her left her companions in danger and her tricky Protector magic didn't allow that. While she was vulnerable if someone wanted to hurt her, and *only* her, if they were a threat to absolutely anyone else in that moment, her magic worked. Couldn't go around her. Couldn't kill her to get her out of the way.

"I'm going to shoot you," Gun Man said, his voice sounding calm and even. He wasn't panicking, or even particularly worried.

That was probably a pretty big hint that he was used to shooting people. Which, on the whole, seemed to place him very firmly in the bad guy category.

"Fair enough," she said. "Remember what I said about the rebound." She inched closer to the camera.

The mist at her feet swirled in gentle eddies as they moved. The cold made her breath visible. The drums sounded louder. And another warning blow of a conch shell echoed through the hills. She was pretty sure that meant the ghosts were close. And that was so terrifying at such a basic level of her soul, she almost couldn't feel the fear anymore. She'd gone beyond being scared into a mental realm of babbling gibberish. She didn't know what they were going to do, how they were going to stop this, or even really *what* this was. She just kept taking those next steps and tried not to hyperventilate.

If Gun Man thought he could scare her with the paltry threat of shooting her when there were *ghosts* approaching, he was sorely mistaken.

When they were within a few feet of the camera, the gun went off. The crack of sound on the windy hill was like the boom of canon fire right next to her ear. Cary winced. Marianne let out a curse. Lucy gasped. Angie didn't make any sound at all. Which Cary might have found interesting if she weren't so scared.

Of the ghosts. The bullet never got close enough to worry her.

Her magic was already in full swing, which meant the bullet slammed into her shield a safe two feet away from Cary and her friends. Rather than rebound, it smashed flat and dropped to the ground in a harmless lump of metal.

"No rebound," she called to the Gun Man. "That worked out for you."

The sound of drums drew nearer. She could feel her breath coming in faster and faster gasps and tried to slow another sharp rise of panic. She couldn't afford to pass out. Not with guns going off and ghosts approaching.

"What the hell?" Gun Man cursed, and shot again.

Another loud crack. The distinct sound of a small lump of metal hitting the damp ground.

"You're wasting bullets," she told him.

Cold seeped into her bones. She was a little worried about the blackness seeping in at the edges of her vision. She took a deep breath in, let it out slowly, tried to ignore the fact that it was icy cold.

"I really hate ghosts," she said aloud.

Three warm, very solid hands touched her shoulders. "We've got you," Lucy said. "We're safe, you're safe, because we're safe."

Cary let out a shaky breath. Lucy was right. She was protecting them. Because of that, she was safe too. It was a weird side effect of her powers, and maybe leaned away from the altruism she might otherwise have been able to claim on this job. But in that moment, she didn't care because she was pretty sure she spotted the glow of approaching ghosts out of the corner of her eye, and all she could think about was not not *not* looking at them.

When they reached the camera, Cary pushed as close to it as she could get. Which pushed the woman behind it backward. That was useful. She moved closer and the woman stumbled back another step from the camera.

"What the hell are you doing?" the woman said. "Stop that. You don't know what you're doing!"

"You could explain how all this works," Cary said. "That would be helpful."

She moved so she was between the camera and the bad guys, giving Lucy a chance to do whatever she was going to do with the camera without the bad guys interfering.

"You can't!" the woman shouted as Lucy took the camera off its tripod. "You'll ruin everything."

"Care to explain everything?" Cary asked again. "And by the way, even if you don't, we're pretty sure you're making an assassination thingy here, or maybe something to kill a lot of people if you put it on a network channel, so I have no sympathy for you at all right now. I don't like ghosts, but they didn't ask to be used this way. They're just going about their business, haunting the dark night, creeping me the fuck out—"

"Escorting dead Hawaiian royalty," Lucy added.

"That," Cary said, pointing over her shoulder at Lucy, "and you want to come along and capture one so it will kill people. That's rude."

She was pretty sure she sounded like an idiot, but she didn't really care. She frequently sounded like a scold and idiot when confronting bad guys—and that only got worse when she was terrified. But she wasn't here to earn their good opinion. They were the bad guys.

Chatty Man stood away from the altar. "We're not trying to kill nobody. What you talking about?"

"Why else capture a ghost that kills with a look in a camera you can point at people?" Cary said, trying to sound reasonable. Her chattering teeth made that difficult.

"That's not what we got paid for," Chatty Man said.

"Shut up," the woman said. To Gun Man, she said, "Shoot them before they ruin everything."

"I tried," he said, sounding more emotional now. Angry. "She's got a shield of some kind."

"Magic?" the woman snapped, facing Cary again. "How?"

Cary gave her a narrow look. "You've been working with a witch to capture ghosts, and you're asking about *my* magic like magic is surprising to you? That's weird." Over her shoulder to Lucy, she said, "Any ideas?" She kept her gaze on the bad guys so she wouldn't accidentally look in the direction of the approaching ghosts. The others were also, very carefully, not looking at the faint glow coming down through the mountains.

"Actually," Lucy said. "There's this switch right here." Something clicked. "Oh, that's easy. I wonder what happens if I break the tape."

"What kind of tape?"

"Video."

"Stop!" the woman roared and tried to launch at them. She hit Cary's shield and got flung backward onto the wet and misty ground on her ass.

First Man helped her back to her feet. "They're almost here," he said.

"What's this about killing people?" Chatty Man said. "They making that up, bra?"

"Sure," First Man said, but he held the woman's gaze as he said it.

Cary did not like that look. To Chatty, she said, "You, uhm, might want to come over here. Close to me."

"Cary…" Angie's voice held all the question without asking anything out loud.

Marianne asked the question out loud. "What the hell are you doing?"

She sighed. "My job." She motioned Chatty closer. "What's your name?" she asked him.

He didn't move, but he was frowning at First Man and the woman. "What's going on?" he asked them.

"The marchers are almost here," the woman hissed. She sat down at the altar. "Get the camera back. Now."

First Man swung toward Cary, but met with the same result as the woman, ending up a few feet away on his ass. The gun went off again. Another crack of sound so loud, Cary winced.

She gestured to Chatty. "You, whatever your name is, you aren't here for the killing part of this job?"

"There's no killing part. That's not what we're getting paid for."

"Shut. Up," Gun Man said, his voice very quiet.

Shit. "You really really need to get closer to me," she said to Chatty. "Cause they're going to kill you soon if you don't."

Chatty glared at the man with the gun. Then the woman who'd started chanting at the altar. And First Man who charged Cary's shield —unsuccessfully—again.

The glow in her peripheral vision grew brighter. The sounds of drums filled the valley in resounding echoes. Another fog horn blow of a conch shell made the hairs on her neck stand up.

Behind her, Lucy said, "I wonder what will happen if I break this."

The sound of the gun going off again made Cary jump…

Because Gun Man wasn't aiming at her anymore.

8

Cary gasped and made to move toward Chatty, but she knew she was already too late. She couldn't reach him in time to get between him and a bullet.

A part of her knew even making the effort would put her friends in danger and that might have stunted her reaction time.

But in the end, it didn't matter. She couldn't move fast enough to save him.

The large video cassette that flew past her shoulder and got between Chatty and the bullet, however, did move fast enough.

Cary blinked a few times as the plastic case shattered in a shower of sharp little black shrapnel and recording tape. Chatty threw himself to the ground, covering his head with his arms.

The cassette had slowed the bullet just enough to give Chatty time to avoid it. It didn't stop it, of course, but the interference redirected it so that it hit the dirt a foot from Chatty.

Cary let out a breath and faced Lucy. "You…"

But Lucy was already moving. Cary watched with a combination of horror and awe as Lucy leapt at Gun Man.

She grabbed his outstretched arm, swung underneath him so her back was to his chest, his arm stretched out straight over her shoulder.

Then with seeming effortlessness, she thrust her free hand up into the man's elbow while pulling his wrist down.

The sound of breaking bone made Cary flinch and her stomach rolled with a punch of nausea.

Gun Man screamed. His gun dropped harmlessly to the ground.

First Man lunged toward Lucy and the dropped gun. Cary opened her mouth to warn her friend, but Lucy was already moving. She swiveled, kicking the gun away into the darkness, then spun to face Gun Man and kicked him in the stomach, which sent him sprawling backward.

She took First Man's hands as he grabbed for her, twisted around so she faced him and his arms were crossed awkwardly, then kicked him in the knee.

He collapsed to the ground with a shouted curse. Lucy released his arms and spun into a roundhouse kick that landed solidly on the side of First Man's head. He hit the ground face first and didn't move.

"Lucy!" Marianne called a warning.

Lucy spun in time to see Gun Man crawling toward something. Likely his gun.

The woman had risen from the altar, her attention on the fight. She picked up the conch shell and aimed, as if she intended on throwing it at Lucy.

Cary was close enough to block that attack, though, adjusting her stance to put herself between Lucy and the woman while still keeping Marianne and Angie safe. The conch shell bounced off Cary's shield and rebounded, hitting the woman in the shoulder.

She glared at Cary. Cary gave her a what-did-you-expect look, before turning to check on the camera which Lucy had dropped to go after Gun Man.

The green lines encircling the video camera moved in frantic chaos now, sizzling and spitting like electrical sparks.

"That doesn't look good," she said to Angie and Marianne, nodding at the camera.

She glanced back toward Lucy. She'd managed to put Gun Man into a strangle hold, kneeling on his back, his head pulled up and back while she had one arm wrapped around his neck and her other arm secured around her first. The whole position didn't look particularly ferocious, but the man was gasping and clawing at her arm, so whatever she was doing, it was working.

Chatty rose from his prone position, staring at Lucy and Gun Man. Cary couldn't tell if he wanted to get involved in the fight, was just watching, or was still in shock from someone shooting at him. He glanced at her, then at the woman who was digging in her backpack again.

"A lot is about to go very wrong," Cary said.

Because the drum sounds were really loud. And now she could hear…chanting? Voices anyway. Sounds that had her nerve endings jumping in fear. The camera looked like it was about to explode. Lucy was outside of Cary's protection fighting—possibly strangling—Gun Man. She couldn't tell by looking at him what Chatty would do. And First Man was twitching and moving again.

Though Cary kind of hoped Lucy had broken his knee. He'd be less trouble if he couldn't walk.

But there was still Gun Man's gun out there in the grass somewhere.

And the ground felt like it was trembling as the night marchers approached.

She couldn't be everywhere at once. She didn't want to leave Marianne and Angie unprotected because the marchers were too near. Angie could probably build a circle to protect her and Marianne from the camera if it exploded, and from the ghosts if they arrived before Cary had them in her protection again. But a witch's protection circle wouldn't do shit for bullets.

The woman pulled something that looked like a night stick from her bag. It wasn't a gun, which was a relief, but it was a long, thick chunk of metal—maybe a big flashlight? Cary couldn't tell—which would cause a lot of damage if swung at another human.

Chatty pushed up to his feet finally, his gaze jumping around the night. The woman charged Lucy, but found herself coming up hard against Cary's shields. Cary couldn't protect Lucy from the two men currently next to her, but she could at least keep the woman from joining in.

"Stop her," the woman shouted. "She's killing him."

Cary raised her brows. "He just shot at one of your people. You want me to stop *her*?"

"She won't kill him," Angie said, sounding infinitely reasonable. "She's very well trained."

"She'll just ensure he's unconscious," Marianne added.

The woman glared at them and raised her night stick-possible flashlight thingy and swung at Cary. It bounced off Cary's shield and sent the woman flailing in the opposite direction.

"Physics is a bitch," Cary said.

She could see her breath way too clearly now. Her lips were tingling with the cold.

"What do we do about the exploding camera?" she asked Angie.

"Duck?" Angie said.

"Helpful."

She looked at Chatty and the woman. She hated protecting bad guys with every fiber of her being, but if the camera exploded, they'd get hurt. She couldn't trust the woman not to attack her, but maybe if she got between them and the camera she could both fend off the woman, keep her from Lucy, *and* somehow block both the woman and Chatty from the explosion.

They only had moments. She couldn't be in four places at once. And the limits of her abilities had never been more obvious.

Or frustrating.

At the least, maybe she could keep Chatty safe. She motioned to him, getting frantic as the sparks jumping off the camera turned to popping sounds and a small, green fire broke out in the center of the contraption.

"Get over here," she said to Chatty. "Unless you want to get caught in the explosion."

"What you...?" He looked at her, looked at the camera, and his eyes widened. "Fuck."

"Come here, damn it."

"You closer to the camera." He looked as if he intended to run back into the mountains. But the marchers were coming from that direction.

Cary looked past him, toward the approaching glow, and realized she could see people inside that glow now. Oh shit. She was looking at them. She wasn't supposed to look at them.

Panicked, she dropped her gaze. Yes, she was probably safe because of Protector mode, but… Terror made her throat tight and she couldn't have moved in that moment if she wanted to.

Suddenly, Lucy was beside her. "Keep your heads down," she said to all of them. "Don't look at the ghosts directly."

The marchers moved up their hill, cresting the grassy expanse like a wave. Chatty threw himself onto the ground again, and buried his face in the dirt, keeping his gaze away from the marchers. The woman looked frantically between the burning camera and the marchers before also throwing herself onto the ground and burying her face. She cursed loud, and for a long time, with her face pressed into the wet grass.

Cary wrapped her arms around her friends and turned her back to the ghosts.

Which was maybe one of the hardest things she'd ever done.

Her skin crawled. The cold made her shiver hard. She could *feel* them passing just behind her, hear the sounds of the drums, the voices chanting, the conch shell sounding another warning. She couldn't hear footsteps, but she felt something brush close enough she squeezed her eyes shut and let out a sound like a screech between her teeth.

"You okay?" Lucy asked, sounding calmer than Cary felt.

"Great. Ghosts at my back. Just great."

Lucy patted her. "You're doing wonderfully. Keep your eyes closed."

"Are you looking? You better not be looking."

"You think I'm an idiot?"

"No."

"Then why did you ask if I was one?"

"Because I'm panicking and terrified."

Pause, then, "Fair enough. I forgive you."

"Thank you. How long is this going to last?"

The sense of danger just behind her made every muscle in her body tight. And to her surprise, the temptation to look nearly got the better of her, because *not* looking seemed even more dangerous to her lizard brain.

"Don't know," Lucy said. She sounded calm, but she moved in tighter to their group hug. "I've never seen the marchers before."

The woman on the ground cursed again. Cary ignored her.

And then, just when Cary was sure her nerves couldn't take any more pressure and strain…

The camera exploded.

9

____

The explosion was a light show of epic proportions. Green flames and sparks, ropes of light like sunbursts, and plastic casing shrapnel shot everywhere.

Cary watched in awed horror as shimmering shapes of green danced over the camera, and a low moan filled the air, competing with the continued sounds of drums. The woman and Chatty were already ducked and had their heads covered because of the ghosts still passing behind them, but they were outside Cary's protection. She had to hope none of the flying shrapnel or…whatever the hell the green stuff oozing from the camera was—what the hell was that?—would hurt them.

"What's the green ooze?" Marianne asked aloud.

"Ectoplasm?" Lucy suggested, her normally high voice quite a bit higher than usual.

Cary shivered. This was not *Ghostbusters*, she reminded herself. Even more importantly, she already knew they hadn't succeeded in catching ghosts in their camera because they'd said so.

Unless they had succeeded and were just being greedy wanting more ghosts?

"Did you catch anything at all inside that camera?" Cary called to the woman as the dancing green flames swirled over the top of the green ooze. All of it glowed brightly in the darkness, but not enough to cut the glow just at the edge of her peripheral vision from the ghosts.

Ah! When would the marchers be gone? She was going to look on accident soon. Or in a panic.

Somewhere behind them were Gun Man and First Man, and she had no idea if they were smart enough to keep their heads ducked, if they might be going for the damned gun again…

"The gun?" she murmured to Lucy.

"Not sure where it is in the dark, but I threw it pretty far. And in the path of the marchers. Pretty sure they can't get at it right now, even if they were conscious. Which neither one was when I rejoined you."

"That's…good. And impressive." Then to the woman, she said, "Well? Did you catch ghosts or not?"

"No! Why the hell you think we're out here tonight?"

"I don't know, do I? Because you wouldn't tell me. This is what you get for not monologuing."

"What the hell are you talking about?"

The woman kept her head ducked, her hands over her head, but Cary got the impression if she had looked up it would be to glare daggers at Cary.

Cary ignored the implied glare. "What's the green ooze then? And is it dangerous? Because it's creeping toward you."

The woman did glance up then, her gaze on the ooze. "Fuck." She scrambled in one direction, hissed—because she was moving toward the marchers and they all knew that was a bad idea—and moved closer to Chatty. Who had not lifted his head, even at the mention of green ooze.

"Hey, Chatty," Cary called. "You okay? Did you get hurt in the explosion?"

"Who da fuck's Chatty?" Chatty called.

Cary let out a breath, relieved he wasn't hurt even if he was the bad guy. "You," she said. "And if you wanted to talk more, I'm a good listener." She was still hoping *someone* would explain all this.

But with the echo of the ghostly drums in her ears and the crawling fear climbing her spine, she wasn't sure she'd be able to pay attention to any monologuing right then anyway.

The ooze continued to move over the grass, reaching the altar almost like slow moving lava. And just as if it had been hit by lava, the altar started to sizzle and burn in green flames.

"Uhm," she said, "I don't think that's good."

"Nope," Angie said. "That ooze needs to be contained."

"How?"

"Still don't know what it is," Angie said. "No idea how to contain it."

"How do we stop this green shit?" Lucy called to the woman and Chatty.

"Fuck if I know," the woman said.

"What?" Cary glared at her, but her head was still down.

"Never had the camera explode before," the woman growled. "That was your fault."

"My fault? How the hell was that *my* fault? I'm not the one pouring green potion into a camera and trying to capture ghosts."

"Shut. Up," Chatty said slowly, without moving his hands from covering his head.

Cary wasn't sure if he was talking to her or the woman but she didn't ask. The glow of the ghosts behind them was beginning to fade.

She wanted to look, to check on their progress, so badly her body trembled. Her muscles ached from the tension of waiting for the marchers to pass without turning to face them. The drums started to fade, and the sounds of chanting ebbed, the next conch shell trumpet echoed from farther away.

Still, that cold cold air turned her breath to smoke and the dance of icy fingers along her spine felt almost physical rather than psychological. She desperately wanted to face the threat rather than keeping her back to it. Every part of her, not just her lizard brain, rebelled at keeping her back to the danger.

The altar popped and sizzled, melting under the green ooze. The flower lei caught fire, burning with the unnatural green light.

Worry about the green oozing goop started to dominate Cary's panicked mind. She needed to do something to stop that disaster—whatever disaster it turned into. But she couldn't do a damned thing until the night marchers passed.

Which meant she had to hope the green goop didn't kill anyone first.

10

$\mathcal{C}$ary counted under her breath, each number matching the rhythm of the still audible drums. They were fading but not fast enough. She bounced on her toes. Waiting and hoping that ooze didn't reach Chatty or the woman before the marchers had finished their…well, their march.

The air began to warm, just a little, enough that she could no longer see her breath hanging like fog in front of her face. She still shivered from residual cold, but at least the breeze was warmer. The rough winds that had proceeded the night marchers had died back and the trees were no longer bent sideways. The glow of ghostly passing faded in her peripheral vision.

Almost time, almost done. She counted from one again, cycling until she reached twenty, before starting over. She wasn't sure why she was counting, but it seemed a good way to tick off the passing moments so she wouldn't lose her mind panicking.

The green ooze had nearly melted all of the altar now. The fire, if it hadn't been green, might have looked cheerful and warm. She realized with that thought that although it was acting like lava, the green ooze didn't seem to be pumping out any heat. At least not that Cary could feel from her position a yard away. She was close enough that if it was

121

warm she would have felt it. She couldn't tell if it was cold, though, because the air hadn't heated enough for that yet.

A loud moan from behind her made her wince. Was that a ghost or one of the two men Lucy had left unconscious?

"Think that was a ghost," Lucy said, leaning into Cary.

Cary made a strangled sort of squeak she had no control over. She couldn't even speak her terror anymore. Even knowing the marchers were moving on, that they'd passed without paying particular attention to any of the living, she kept waiting for the "gotcha" moment, when a ghost popped up right in front of her to claim her soul. Or something. She didn't honestly know what scared her so much. Just…ghosts.

"Almost past," Angie said, sounding as if she were reassuring herself as much as she was Cary.

"You scared of ghosts, too?" Cary asked. "A big bad witch like you?"

"Ha. And not as scared as you are. But I can't say as I like them. I'm glad I'm not a medium, let's put it that way."

"Wow," Marianne said. "I didn't think you were afraid of anything."

"Oh, yeah, I have my fears," Angie said. "But only a few left at this stage. Face hell often enough, and you get kind of used to it."

"That's gonna require more explaining," Lucy said.

"One day," Angie said. "Maybe."

"Huh?" Cary said, because there were still ghosts behind them, even if farther away now, and that was the best she could do to contribute to the conversation.

"What are we going to do about the ooze?" Lucy said. "That's well outside my skillset. I'm not sure the river spirit counted on us accidentally blowing up the ghost catching camera."

"The woman pretty much confirmed that's what it is," Marianne said, "when she said they hadn't caught a ghost yet."

"So destroying it was good," Angie said. "Probably exactly what Lucy and Cary were supposed to do to atone for Cary being here."

"Except it's now oozing green lava that we don't know how to stop," Lucy pointed out.

"Lava that isn't hot," Cary murmured. "Yet it burned through that entire altar."

"Noticed that," Angie said. "Wonder if that's a clue how to stop it."

"I don't have any water on hand," Lucy said. "That's how you slow lava. Spray the hell out of it until everyone is out of its way. Then let it roll. You can't really stop it. Just slow it down."

"But this isn't real lava," Angie said.

"And it's not hot," Cary repeated.

"It was a witch's potion, according to our bad guys," Lucy said. "Would magic stop it?"

"Might," Angie said, "if I knew what the hell it was and how it was made and what spells went into it. I don't have a clue. I've never encountered ghost trapping spells before."

"You got anything in your purse that might stop it?" Lucy asked Marianne.

Marianne could do amazing things with material, not just magic pockets and weaving straw into gold—though she could do all that. Cary had once seen her transport someone with a piece of material. And pull a loom out of another flat piece of material like a magic trick. If anyone had a piece of material on hand that might stop magic ghost catching ooze, it was Marianne.

"Nothing that will stop that," Marianne said, sounding annoyed by this fact. "But I swear I'm gonna figure out something that will and keep it on hand for all future adventures with you three."

"You can't prepare for everything," Angie said philosophically.

"But I can try," Marianne said.

"You hear that?" Lucy asked.

Everyone stilled. It took Cary a moment to realize what Lucy was talking about.

"The drums… They've stopped." And despite all her fears, Cary turned around in a circle, checking the area for the marchers.

They seemed to be gone.

Relief like a physical weight dropped onto Cary's shoulders, and she nearly fell to her knees from the sensation.

"And no one died," Lucy said. "That's good."

"That is excellent," Cary said, still trying to remain upright as her knees wobbled.

"We still have magic green ooze to deal with," Angie reminded them.

The woman and Chatty both finally raised their heads. Chatty scrambled to his feet and moved away from the ooze, but in a direction opposite Cary, so she couldn't keep him safe from the stuff.

"You might want to come over here behind me," she said to him. "Just, you know, to be safe."

"You're closer to that. I'm going this way." He moved another few paces in the opposite direction.

Cary sighed. She couldn't keep someone safe if they didn't let her. Which was a super frustrating part of her job. Almost as frustrating as not being able to *do* anything to the bad guys besides stand in their way.

"So," Lucy said, "what do we do with the ooze? We can't…put it back."

"And physical contact seems like a bad idea anyway," Angie said, nodding at the sizzling grass around it. "That's gonna leave a mark."

"Is it just me, or does it seem like its seeping into the ground around the altar?" Cary tilted her head to one side as she studied the stuff. It hadn't moved very far beyond the spot the altar had been.

The woman, on her feet now, had backed up with Chatty. He nudged her. "What we gonna do about that?"

"Not my fault," she said, defensive. "Go get the gun." She glared at Cary and Lucy. "Check on the other two."

"Bad idea," Lucy said. "No guns. They're dangerous."

"What you gonna do about it?" Chatty asked as he moved toward the two fallen men.

Lucy sighed. "Did you not see what I did to your colleagues? Were you not even paying attention? I swear." She looked at Cary. "This is the problem with being a teacher sometimes. Students just don't pay attention."

"Shame," Cary said. "Stay away from the ooze while you kick his ass. We'll work on a way to contain the stuff."

"Fair enough." Lucy trotted toward the two men she'd already knocked unconscious.

Cary realized she could just see their bodies on the ground still. And neither was moving. She had a moment's qualms—Lucy had *just* knocked them out, right?—but then she realized Lucy was so well trained she would never accidentally kill someone. On purpose…yeah, sure. But not on accident. If all she'd wanted to do was ensure they were unconscious, that's all she'd have done.

The woman glared at Cary as Chatty went to find the gun and face Lucy's wrath.

"So," Angie said, "ooze. What do we think?"

"That it's sinking into the ground now," Marianne said. "Not sure that's good."

"What the hell is it?" Cary asked the woman. "And do you have a name? I'm getting really tired of thinking of you as 'the woman'."

"Fuck you," the woman said.

"That's an interesting name. Hippy parents?"

The woman snarled.

"Fine." Cary let out a breath. Couldn't say she didn't try.

Despite her snarling and tossing around orders to Chatty, the woman did take another few steps away from the ooze, her gaze darting between it, Cary's group, and Chatty—who'd reached one of the fallen men. Lucy bounced on her toes a little ways from him. She'd put herself between him and the direction she'd tossed the gun. But she didn't attack first. She just stood there, a little like Cary usually did, and waited for Chatty to make the first move.

"What happens if this stuff sinks into the ground?" Cary asked the woman—she couldn't really call her Fuck You in her head, though a part of her kind of wanted to.

"Fuck should I know," the woman said. "I told you I don't know what it is."

"What kind of spell did you get from the witch?" Angie asked. "That will help."

"Why would I want to help you? You ruined everything."

"Yeah, still not sure what that everything is, since you won't tell us, so I'm not losing any sleep over it," Cary said. Her annoyance was returning quickly now that there were no ghosts passing within a few feet of her. She shivered at the memory. The remembered sensation of cold and the hair-raising knowledge that they'd just been right *there* behind her was going to haunt her. No pun intended.

"Stuff's still soaking into the ground," Marianne said.

"What will it do if it soaks in fully?" Cary asked Angie, but loud enough the woman could hear.

"Got me. Hopefully just keep sinking. Might leave a…a poltergeist spot here."

"A what?"

"A spot that attracts lost souls. Maybe opens a gateway to the half-realm that ghosts inhabit. No way for me to know without knowing the base spell."

"A gateway sounds very bad," Cary said. "I'm pretty sure we haven't made this situation better."

"Well, that depends on their original plan, too, doesn't it?" Marianne said. "If they were going to commit mass murder with a ghost camera, then a single spot that may or may not open a doorway to the ghost realm seems the better of the two outcomes."

"Any way to mark the ground?" Cary asked. "Keep people from stepping on the spot?"

The ooze had almost fully sunk into the ground now, but the soil around it was glowing a ghastly green color that didn't look at all natural. Maybe the glow would be enough to keep people away. Or, given human curiosity, it would more likely attract people and some bonehead would decide they needed to dig here to find out what it was.

A stench like rotten flesh and burnt grass rose from the spot now, a smell that hadn't been there before. Up to that point, Cary realized, the ooze hadn't actually smelled like much at all.

"If the glow doesn't keep people away, the smell will," Marianne said, putting a hand over her mouth and nose.

Lucy tsked loudly enough to draw their attention. Cary glanced her way. Chatty was on his back in the grass, Lucy standing a few feet away shaking her head at him.

"I told you that was a bad idea," Lucy said in full instructor mode now. "You can't just charge someone and assume your superior size will be the only advantage you need. Now, up. Try again. This time, balancing on the balls of your feet, knees bent."

Cary almost laughed. The woman snarled at Chatty and Lucy, and started toward them.

"Got another one coming in," Cary called to warn Lucy.

"No problem," Lucy said as Chatty charged her. She stepped to one side and gave him what looked like a gentle shove. He flew a few feet forward and face-planted into the grass.

The woman screamed and raced toward Lucy. Lucy didn't even turn to face her. She just stood there, staring at Chatty as he tried to rise to his feet. At the last moment, she squatted down just a little, but it was enough to throw the woman off balance as she reached for Lucy and grasped only empty air. Lucy rose up, taking hold of the woman's outstretched arm as she did, flipping the woman over her shoulder, and the woman hit the ground on her back at Lucy's feet. The resounding thud when she landed made Cary wince.

"You good?" Cary asked, knowing Lucy had them handled.

"Of course. How's the ooze?"

"Sinking into the ground."

"That doesn't sound good."

Lucy took a few steps back when the woman rolled onto her stomach and scrambled back to her feet. She charged Lucy again, this time in a way that seemed a lot more coordinated. She grasped at Lucy, catching her by the shirt, and tried to spin her around. Lucy did a duck and turn thing that put her under the woman's arms again, twisting her arms in the process. There was a tear of material as Lucy's shirt ripped. But then the woman ended up on her back again, in a move Cary hadn't even been able to follow.

"I'll fix your shirt for you," Marianne said. "Don't worry about the rip."

"Thank you," Lucy called. She danced out of the woman's reach when she tried to grab Lucy's legs.

Chatty raced forward again. He swung a big fist at her head. She ducked under the swing and hit him with the palm of her hand in the center of his chest. The gesture looked like it wouldn't cause much damage to someone of Chatty's thickness, but the man gasped and dropped to the ground, sucking in air.

"Ooze has fully sunk into the ground now," Angie said calmly.

"Probably bad, that, huh?" Cary said, her attention divided between Lucy's fight and the glowing spot of grass that marked the ooze's location. "Would a containment circle keep that from causing trouble?"

"Might," Angie said, nodding slightly. "Might just. I don't have the stuff I'd need to make it permanent, but we could come back later and do that. Give me a chance to check with a local witch and see if there's anything we'd need specific to the islands. Hell, a local witch might be able to set the circle or figure a way to extract the ooze safely."

"You still doing okay?" Cary called to Lucy when Lucy took a sucker punch to the shoulder. She'd been in midmotion so that's all Chatty got with his awkward swing. But given his girth and the size of his fist, Cary still worried.

"I'm good," Lucy said, sounding entirely too cheerful as she danced away from another awkward Chatty swing and the woman diving at her feet.

To Cary's untrained—or barely trained because she kept having to work when she had training sessions with Lucy—that lunging at Lucy's feet move didn't look very effective.

"She loves this shit," Marianne said with a head shake. "And she's playing with them. None of them trained to fight."

"Still," Cary said, "Chatty's got some big arms on him. He catches her with another sucker punch in the wrong place…"

"She's got this," Marianne said. "You gonna do the circle?" she asked Angie.

"Yeah. Think that's our only option now. Temporary fix but it'll have to do."

Angie began murmuring under her breath, doing some intricate weaving of fingers and hands, a series of gestures which Cary knew were part of the spell she was building but not entirely sure what each gesture meant. Secret witch knowledge, Angie had told her with a smile. The books she'd been studying on witchcraft didn't clarify anything either. Apparently, some aspects of witchcraft had to be learned in a master-apprentice relationship and were never written down. Just as well, Cary thought, looking at that glowing spot on the ground where the green ooze had disappeared. Magic wasn't something amateurs should mess with.

"That first guy is getting up," Marianne called to Lucy.

"Thanks," Lucy called back, readjusting her stance to keep First Man in view while she spun the woman in a circle that sent her careening off in a direction back toward Cary and the others.

Gun Man still seemed to be down, but with First Man recovering, Cary was a little worried Gun Man was pretending to be unconscious, waiting to move on Lucy.

Lucy was perfectly capable of tossing all four people around. She'd specifically trained for years in techniques that allowed a single combatant to fight multiple opponents at once—it was a popular style used at both exhibitions and at competitions at Lucy's level. It helped if the other people actually knew what they were doing and could fight. When they were like these four, none of them trained in martial arts, Lucy said it was a bit trickier because they kept getting in each other's way and weren't as predictable. Still, Cary had personally seen her do this more than once. She knew Lucy was able for the fight itself.

But there was still that damned gun out there somewhere.

"How goes the circle?" she asked Angie quietly.

Angie didn't answer as she was still murmuring her spell. So Cary took that as an "I'm still working on it" and said to Marianne, "I'm getting nervous about the missing gun."

"Not an unfounded worry," Marianne said. "Once Angie's done, you want to go look for it?"

"Yeah. And also get close enough to Lucy to keep her safe from gunfire."

"Fair point."

"What are we going to do with these guys?" Cary asked, not really expecting an answer. They weren't police. They couldn't arrest them. Basically, the best they could do was let them run away and report the less supernatural parts of this to the cops tomorrow morning. And hope the cops didn't accidentally stumble into whatever that ooze was creating in the grass.

"Circle's up," Angie said, her voice a little strained.

That was strange enough, Cary faced her. "What's wrong?"

"Well." She frowned. "Circle's good and solid, small and should last a couple of days so long as it's not disturbed by something like a cat, but..."

When she paused and her eyes widened, Cary actually felt her breath catch. A cold shiver crawled along her spine. She didn't want to look. But she couldn't *not* look either.

She turned to face the glowing green spot where the ooze had vanished.

And came face-to-face with a ghost.

11

The ghost was a glowing, greenish color, like the ooze, and transparent enough to see the trees through its torso. The entity was vaguely male shaped, though it was hard to tell. Vaguely human shaped at any rate. Not many of the details of the thing were clear, a head with a wide open mouth, long hair around indistinct shoulders and body. The eyes in the head were white, which was super scary against the green glow. The open mouth may or may not have been issuing a sound. Cary couldn't tell.

Her pulse was rushing too hard in her ears from fear for her to hear anything.

"Uhm," Marianne said. "What?"

Which was better than Cary could do. Her throat had locked up the minute she faced those white eyes.

"Not a marcher," Angie said. "I think."

"Hope not," Cary squeaked.

"Yeah, cause wouldn't we be dying now?" Marianne asked.

"Cary's protecting us," Angie said. "We should be fine."

Cary didn't feel fine. And she wasn't confident they'd be fine. And Angie's slight hesitance hadn't helped that feeling at all. But most of that thinking process went on in the part of her brain that still functioned.

A very small part of her brain.

Currently subsumed under her internal screaming terror.

Ghosts couldn't be stopped with physical force. They weren't substantial. Lucy couldn't hit one and knock it out. Marianne didn't have ghost stopping cloth in her purse. Angie wasn't a medium and didn't do ghost magic. They stood maybe three feet from the ghost. Whose mouth was open and it looked like it might be moaning. And every brain cell in Cary's head demanded she turn and run away as fast as her legs would carry her.

She didn't. Mostly because she could no longer feel her legs. But boy, did she want to run away.

"Circle?" Cary wheezed. Pushing air over her windpipes was an awful lot of effort.

"Seems to be holding it," Angie said. "Wasn't built for ghost containment, but for ooze containment. And since that seems to have been called by the ooze…think it'll work."

"Still love to know for sure what they'd intended to do with that camera," Marianne said. Her voice was barely above a whisper. She could form sentences, which impressed the hell out of Cary, but the words trembled.

"Lucy?" Cary managed.

She couldn't drag her gaze away from the ghost long enough to check on her, but there was that small, still functioning part of her brain that was aware her dear friend was out there in the dark fighting possibly four people and a gun in the grass somewhere and Lucy wasn't inside Cary's protection.

And there was another ghost.

"Still holding her own," Angie said. "Luce, you good?"

"Yup." There was a thud. A gasp. Another curse that wasn't Lucy's sweet voice. "How'd you call another ghost?"

"Not sure. Circle. Ooze. Hard to tell."

"You okay, Cary?"

Lucy's concern for her while in the middle of a fight was both touching and a little appalling. Cary was supposed to be a Protector, not some damsel in distress from a gothic novel ready to charge off into the moors like an idiot. Oh, she felt like a damsel in distress in a gothic novel ready to charge off into the moors like an idiot. But she wasn't *supposed* to be that woman.

"Managing," she said. Which was true because she hadn't bolted yet and she counted that as a win.

She'd thought having the night marchers walking behind them had been scary. Somehow, facing and seeing the ghost, having them moan silently just a few feet away, had fried her brain even more thoroughly than knowing, but not seeing, the marchers.

When the ghost pointed a long bone of a finger at her, she had such an overwhelming urge to scream, she hurt her teeth clenching her jaw to hold it in.

Sound of some kind escaped her, but she wasn't sure anyone— herself included—could have interpreted the sound as anything that made sense.

"We gonna die since we're looking at it," Marianne called to Lucy.

"Not a marcher," Lucy said. "I don't think anyway." A grunt. Another thud. Someone gasped for breath. The distinct sound of a body hitting the ground hard. "No drums."

"What…what then?" Cary stammered. It was a full question and more than one word so she was pretty proud of herself.

"Another restless spirit," Angie said. The words were casual, but she didn't sound her usual matter-of-fact self.

If even Angie was a little freaked out, that couldn't be good.

"Why's it pointing at Cary?" Marianne asked.

Which was a good question. And also a terrifying fact.

"Got me," Angie said.

"Helpful," Cary said, but her voice was so choked she wasn't sure anyone would hear her.

Maybe it was pointing at her because she wasn't supposed to be in the islands, like the dragon-woman had said. Maybe it was mad at her for being here. Maybe it was personally offended by her bringing her brand of magic to Hawaii.

Or maybe it was just pointing at the person standing closest to it, which was Cary since she was between it and Marianne and Angie.

And then, as if they didn't have enough going on in that moment, from the distance, Cary heard the sound of sirens.

"Cops," Marianne guessed.

"Someone must have heard the earlier gunshots," Angie said.

"How are we going to explain a ghost?" Marianne asked.

"Got me," Angie said again.

"Should we…leave?" Cary wasn't sure she could even if she wanted to. Especially because the ghost might be dangerous to the police. Despite her lizard brain demanding she run away, her Protector instincts overrode that desire. She might not be able to move to protect Lucy, but she could continue to stand here and protect everyone from a ghost.

Which was still pointing at her.

But, she realized quite suddenly, she wasn't freezing cold. She couldn't feel that icy brush of ghostly breeze on her skin. The wind hadn't kicked up. She wasn't smelling anything strange. Not even the rotten flesh smell of the ooze—and wasn't that a relief! Just ordinary cool breeze, the scents of tropical forest and the faint hint of salt in the damp air.

"The circle…" She swallowed to wet her dry mouth as she attempted to string a few words together. "Seems to be." Another gulp. "Working. No cold."

"She's right," Marianne said suddenly. "No cold."

"Can't smell the ooze either," Angie said.

"Must be working," Lucy said from just behind them.

Cary startled enough to finally look away from the ghost. She blinked a few times at Lucy. Then glanced behind her. One of the four bad guys was laid out on the grass, but the other three were gone.

"Uh?" she asked. The ghost still glowed green in her peripheral vision, but when she wasn't looking directly into its white eyes, she could manage a little more coherence. Just not much.

"They ran away when they heard the sirens," Lucy said with a shrug. "Deeper into the mountains. That one—" she pointed at the person still sprawled in the grass, "—is out cold. I'm sure the cops will have a lot of questions for him."

"Which one?"

"The one who'd been whispering to the woman. The white guy with blond hair."

"Not the gunman?" Cary said. If she focused on Lucy and not the still hovering ghost, she could almost talk. That was definite progress.

"Nope, 'fraid he ran off with the others."

"Did he ever find the gun?" Angie asked.

"No," Lucy said, "none of them did. It's still out there somewhere."

"Kind of glad that's not Chatty," Cary said.

"He was just as much of an asshole as the others," Lucy said.

"Yeah, but he wasn't out here to kill anyone and didn't seem to know what the real plan had been. The cops will get more out of that guy." Cary gestured to unconscious man.

Just then flashlights appeared in the distance, from the direction of the main ranch building.

"How we going to explain that?" Marianne pointed at the ghost.

"Uhm." Cary had nothing. Having to explain things to the authorities was something she tried really hard to avoid.

"Could we claim its some weird special effect?" Angie asked, lowering her voice as the flashlights got closer, accompanied by the sound of cops shouting. "Something to do with the group that was here?"

"You want them to disturb your circle?" Lucy asked.

"Yeah, that would be bad," Cary said, watching the police approach now. They were close enough to see the ghost.

"We could just tell them it's a ghost," Lucy said.

"That gonna get us arrested and thrown into a padded cell?" Marianne asked.

"If they're looking at the same thing we're looking at, I'm not sure how they could call us crazy," Lucy said. "They'll either make up their own excuses, or maybe even try to cover up what they're looking at if they don't believe it's a ghost."

"Or they'll believe it's a ghost and avoid that spot appropriately," Angie said.

"Either way, we're about to find out." Cary raised her hands in the air as the cops approached, guns and flashlights raised.

"What's going on out here?" a deep voice from behind one of the flashlights demanded.

"You want to take this?" Cary asked Lucy since she was the local.

"Thanks," she muttered at Cary under her breath.

But then she stepped forward, her hands up, and started explaining everything to the cops. The only thing she left out was the part about the dragon-woman spirit sending them here—she claimed they'd just been out for a night hike so she could show her mainland friends the stars, and they'd stumbled across the four with the camera and been held at gunpoint.

"Where's the gun now?" one of the cops demanded.

Lucy shrugged. "In the grass back there somewhere. And one of the men is still there. The others ran away."

Cops scattered around the hill top. A few went to the fallen man. A few more moved past him—Cary presumed to search for the gun. Another three continued to hold their guns on Cary and her friends, flashlights right in Cary's eyes. She squinted against the brightness, but couldn't complain. The light kept her from seeing the ghost in her peripheral vision.

"That's not a real ghost," one of the cops said. Sounding about as sure as a person staring at ghost could sound.

"You evah seen a ghost?" another one asked.

"No," the first said.

"Well now you have."

"Bullshit."

But the response lacked conviction.

Cary could relate.

12

The cops arrested the unconscious man. Found the gun. And took Cary and her friends to a nearby police station to give statements.

None of the officials actually admitted to seeing the ghost after that one passing exchange just after the police arrived, even though it had still been floating there, glowing green and scary, as the cops took everyone away. Despite the denial, not a single cop got too near Angie's circle or the ghost, and in fact actively avoided the spot.

Cary had avoided looking at the entity again too. She didn't want to know if it continued to point at her.

One or two of the cops crossed themselves. A few others made similar protective gestures that Cary didn't recognize. But no one came out and discussed the ghost out loud.

By the time the sun rose, Lucy had convinced the police they were innocent bystanders, just out for a hike. Between her petit cuteness and her little girl's voice, she charmed at least three of the police officers so thoroughly, they were bringing her food and drink and hovering over her protectively throughout the questioning.

Cary kept her amusement to herself, but she was pretty impressed.

Thanks to Lucy's superb handling of the local law enforcement, they learned that the man taken into custody was a wanted man, with ties to drug runners. The cops assumed the four had been out in the hills setting up a drug exchange or something of the kind. They didn't have an explanation for the broken, burnt camera.

The ghosts went unremarked on.

By the time Cary and her friends returned to Lucy's dads' house, she was exhausted and figured she'd have to sleep for the day. They still had several days before the wedding, so she hoped no one would mind.

She still had no idea what the bad guys had intended to do with the camera and the marchers. Which bugged her. She hated not understanding. But for that morning anyway, she wasn't getting answers and she really needed to sleep.

THE NEXT EVENING, AFTER CONSULTING A LOCAL WITCH, ANGIE, THE resident witch, and a medium returned to the Kualoa hills behind the ranch to settle the ghost and set some protections around the area that would keep the ooze from causing more trouble.

Cary did not go with them because…ghosts.

Instead, she returned to the Byodo-In Temple while Lucy and Marianne dealt with Lucy's dads' last minute planning crisis—a menu change to accommodate someone's allergies they hadn't known about.

She went directly to the meditation spot by the little waterfall.

The sun had moved close to the horizon when she arrived, leaving the area deeply shadowed, the buzz of mosquitos louder, and the sounds of tourists faint. There were only two other groups at the Temple since it was closing to the public soon.

Trickling water added a nice background music as the breeze gently blew a rich flower and forest scent over Cary's face.

She waited in silence, sitting on the pentagonal wooden bench in the center of the mediation temple.

The dragon emerged from the water about fifteen minutes later.

Cary rose to greet the spirit as she took on a human form. She was once against dressed in a green-blue swath of shimmering material that looked like the ocean, her crown of flowers and palm fronds sat low on her brow. The Kukui nut lei around her neck looked darker in the faint light. Her expression was neutral as she stared at Cary, but none of the menace of their earlier encounter emanated from her this time. Cary supposed that was good. Hopefully, the spirit forgave her now for accidentally bringing forbidden magic to the islands.

"What were they trying to do?" Cary asked.

"You stopped them."

It wasn't a question, but Cary said, "Yes."

"Do you have to know what they planned?"

"I suppose it's not necessary to the turning of the world. But it'll bug me if I don't know."

The dragon-woman stared at her in silence long enough, she assumed she wasn't getting her hoped-for explanation.

"Angie and some other witches have gone to settle the spirit that accidentally got called and trapped," she told the dragon-woman.

"I'm aware." Another pause. "They were going to use the marcher they trapped in the camera to kill. To kill more."

"Mass murder?" The network attention. That had been her guess but it seemed so…huge. And the drug dealer ties didn't seem to work into that story very clearly.

"Not at first," the dragon-woman said. "But…eventually."

"What did the drugs have to do with it? Do you know what the plan was long term?"

"To use the camera to kill. To make more if the first worked. They were paid to capture the ghost and test the camera on one of the drug dealers one of the men worked with."

"They didn't all know the camera was a weapon." Cary thought about Chatty, and how he'd denied that possibility.

"No. The full extent of the plan was known to only one of the four."

"What happens to the three who got away?"

"Others will take care of them. I have many warriors."

Cary nodded. "So…have we atoned for my presence? Is Lucy safe here now?"

"You have." The dragon-woman paused and then, "She always was. Had *you* not proven worthy, you would have been punished. But I will have words with the Fae who create Protectors. They neglected their duty not telling you your magic wasn't allowed in these islands."

"Yeah, I'm gonna have a talk with them about that too," she said dryly. "But Lucy's safe, right?" This was a very important point for her and she needed to be absolutely certain. She'd hate to never be allowed back to Hawaii. The place was fantastic and she loved it here—even with the side excursion to rescue ghosts—but she'd stay away if she had to.

"Lucy is one of ours. She is welcome."

"She's not Hawaiian."

"She's not. But I'm willing to make allowances for a strong heart."

Which was a very good way to describe Lucy. "You sent others to stop these people before I arrived?"

"Yes. And some died."

"So… Then it was kind of handy I arrived uninvited and you could use my Protector powers to help. Right?"

The dragon-woman stared at her without answering.

"Can I come back if Lucy invites me, or do I have to stay away from now on?"

Another long silent stare, and Cary was certain she'd be banned. Ah well. At least she'd gotten here once.

Then the dragon-woman said, "You will be allowed back. But only you. And we will reserve the right to call on you again, should we need the help of a Protector."

"Fair enough." She worked hard not to get too excited, but her happiness leaked into her voice. She'd have hated being banned. "But…why don't you and the North American Fae work together to make Protectors for Hawaii?"

"That is a discussion beyond your…province."

Cary snorted. Not the first time she'd been told something was none of her business. People told her that all the time. Several times in the last few days, as a matter of fact. But to be fair, she'd gotten more answers from the dragon-woman than she'd expected, so she couldn't even argue.

"Is that all you sought, Protector? Answers."

"That. And to make sure Lucy was safe now. Though I'd also like to make sure the danger isn't ongoing. We did stop them, didn't we?"

"You did. Their plan will not come to fruition now."

"Those with the money who paid for this originally?"

"As I said. They will be seen to."

"Do I want to know?"

"No. And I wouldn't tell you anyway."

Cary sighed. Her part was done and she was being dismissed. Which was a little irritating, but not even a little surprising. All that really mattered, though, was that Lucy was safe. The rest she'd leave to the Hawaiian spirits to take care of.

"Any messages for Lucy before I go?" she asked. Darkness rolled down the mountains, filling in the area. Lights from the Temple flickered to life and it sounded like someone was coming to chase her out of the area.

"Give her my thanks for her assistance," the dragon-woman said. "I shall see her again if I need her." She dropped back into the stream without changing shapes, disappearing into the water just as a staff member cleared the slight hill.

"We're closed to visitors now," the woman said, her tone polite but firm.

"Sorry," Cary said. "Lost track of time. It's very…peaceful here."

The woman smiled and hovered, waiting to ensure Cary did leave.

She glanced back at the trickling waterfall before descending the stone steps. A larger than usual lizard sat on one of the rocks. Not a dragon, this time. Just a very big lizard. It flickered its forked tongue out at her once.

Cary gave it a nod and turned back to the path, eager to get back to her friends.

Hopefully with no more work detours.

She'd had more than enough ghosts for one vacation.

CARY AND THE DEMON WITCH

When her best friend's mysterious past comes calling…

Cary Redmond is prepared to step in.

Although powerful witch, Angie Jordan, is one of Cary's closest friends, there are parts of Angie's past she refuses to talk about. Things she's hinted at but always avoids explaining. Demon related things. And while Cary is very curious about that past, she also respects her friend's privacy. After all, everyone should be allowed their secrets.

But when someone out of Angie's past comes to town and threatens her family, Cary doesn't hesitate to throw herself between this threat and her friend. She might not understand the undertone, but she can keep Angie and her family from getting hurt. After all, it's her job as a magical Protector.

And what good is being a magical Protector if you can't stand between your friends and disaster?

1

C ary sat on her back porch, idly tossing a soggy tennis ball to
her mundane terrier-collie cross, Fred, with one hand and held
her steaming cup of coffee in the other. The scent of fresh roasted hazel
nut drifted up and scented the late winter air. Though cold, it was the
first dry day they'd had in a week, and she intended to take advantage
of it by being outside.

Her basset hound, Pickles, who was actually a foo-lion, rested on
the porch next to her, flopped into her basset sprawl, her jowls spread
out around her nose. The third dog that made up her little pack, Buck, a
golden Lab who was really a demon dog, sniffed the fence border,
mostly ignoring Fred as he tore across the lawn.

A bright blue sky overhead and the sharp cold air contrasting with
her warm coffee mug made her sigh. This was a rare moment of peace
in her ordinarily strange life and she savored it.

The life of a magical Protector was…interesting. But more in the
curse meaning of that word. She lived in Interesting Times, and that
wasn't necessarily a good thing. Becoming a walking Kevlar vest,
whose entire job description was "jump in between good guys and bad
guys and keep the good guys safe," using magic she didn't actually

control but which flowed through her thanks to her bosses, had been eye opening.

At least it paid well.

After doing this job for a few years, though, she was almost used to the magical world she hadn't known existed before becoming a Protector. Demons, vampires, shapeshifters, witches and wizards... Sometimes she just had to shake her head. What the mundane human world didn't know. It was probably better they didn't know about all the otherworldly stuff going on around them all the time anyway. Humans were a jumpy and reactive species. And not all of those witches and wizards and shapeshifters and such were bad.

Her cellphone rang, breaking into her quiet. She sighed and dug it out of her coat pocket. Probably her mother. Her bosses didn't do anything so ordinary as call her on the phone when they had a job for her. If this was work related, they would have just appeared in her backyard. Or sent her ever-annoying faery mentor, Jaxer, to tell her she had work to do.

She looked at the screen, a little surprised by the name that flashed up in white block letters. Speaking of one of the good witches...

"Angie, hey, what's up?" she answered, worry creeping into her tone.

Angela Jordan was a powerful witch and one of Cary's best friends. It wasn't unusual for Angie to call at random times during the day. But she had family in town visiting at the moment, so Cary hadn't expected to hear from her for at least another week.

"Can you come over right now?" Angie asked. "Lucy is on her way after her last class and Marianne is due in half an hour, after she closes her shop."

"What's wrong?" Cary stood and hurried inside, motioning the dogs to follow. Because Pickles and Buck came inside immediately, Fred followed without her having to nag him. "Is it your family? Is something wrong?"

"Not exactly." Angie sighed. "Just a sec." Then she called to someone, "I'll be down in a minute. Just making a call. It's work related." She came back to Cary. "Sorry about that."

"Is this work related?"

Angie owned a successful psychic readings business she ran out of her own home. The business thrived because Angie actually was psychic, as well as being a witch. Most of her clients were mundane humans, and according to Angie, were more in need of a therapist than a real psychic, but Angie was good at listening and that was what really made her so successful.

Cary couldn't imagine what issue had come up relating to Angie's business that would require her to call in reinforcements, but Cary had learned over the last few years that life often turned up thing she couldn't imagine.

She locked the back door—even though technically she didn't have to. Between the glamour on her house that kept people away who weren't invited, and the presence of a demon dog and a foo lion, no one could break into her home. But she locked the doors anyway because some habits were impossible to break, and her dad had instilled door-locking into her too thoroughly to be disregarded now.

"Not work…exactly," Angie said. "It's a long story. But I need some help to keep my family occupied while I sort this out, and that help needs to be comfortable with magic and mayhem." She dropped her voice into a near whisper, making her already deep voice even deeper. "And with my family here, I could use a Protector around. Just in case."

"I'll be there in twenty minutes if I don't get stuck in traffic."

"Thanks."

Angie disconnected just as Cary grabbed her keys off the hook near the front door and headed down the side hall that led to her garage. She called a goodbye to the dogs and hurried out, her stomach tight with worry.

If Angie, of all people, needed a Protector, something was very very wrong.

2

Cary reached Angie's neighborhood in good time, having gotten a remarkable stretch of green lights on the way here. She might have thought something magical was at work, but Angie had told her already she couldn't control traffic lights with magic.

Lucy climbed out of her little Volkswagen Bug across the street as Cary pulled up behind one of two rental cars parked outside Angie's house—Cary assumed the rentals belonged to Angie's family. Marianne's sporty BMW rolled past, and she waved at Cary before pulling into a spot a few houses down on the same side of the road as Lucy had parked.

They converged on the sidewalk at the base of Angie's long front yard. A stone path bisected the neatly trimmed lawn, leading up to Angie's short, narrow front porch. The two story Craftsman house looked undisturbed, which was a relief. Still, Cary's gut was tight with worry.

"What's happening?" Marianne asked, also looking up at the house. She was dressed as elegantly as always in a pair of perfectly tailored wide-legged trousers and a button up silk shirt in an autumnal orange color that complimented her dark skin. As a seamstress, business owner, and magical weaver, Marianne saw it as part of her job to dress so that other people trusted her to dress them. She was wildly successful at it.

"Not sure," Cary said. "Angie didn't elaborate on the phone."

"I got the impression it isn't good, whatever it is," Lucy said in her little girl's voice. Her curly red hair was piled on top of her head in a messy bun, and she was still wearing the simple white gi with a black belt circling her waist that she typically wore when teaching beginner classes at her dojo. She'd obviously rushed over right from her class without bothering to change first.

Which meant Cary wasn't the only one worried about Angie.

The front door to the house opened and Angie stepped out onto the porch, closing the door behind her.

Angie was six foot tall and slim as a supermodel. Today she was dressed in her "street" clothes, jeans and a simple, emerald cowl-neck sweater that showed off her long neck. Her wavy light brown hair was pulled back into a French twist and her makeup was minimal. When working, she dressed in flowing velvet skirts and elaborate hippy shirts with layers of tinkling jewelry on her wrists and ankles and beads woven into her hair, because that's what her clients expected of a psychic. When she wasn't working, though, she preferred business casual or jeans, and the only jewelry she wore were her ever present moon earrings—a present from her brothers in honor of her love of astronomy.

They hurried up the walk to her as she came down the two wooden steps of her porch. She was barefoot, despite the cold, and that made Cary shiver.

"What's wrong?" she asked when she was close enough she didn't have to shout.

"Long story," Angie said with a sigh. "The short version is I've had an issue with this particular witch for years, and she's shown up here in Portland, and it's a thing."

"Is she attacking you?" Marianne asked quietly, looking over her shoulder toward the street.

Angie had a protective circle around her house, something she'd set up when she moved in and fixed into the ground with a literal ring of salt around the periphery. She gave her neighbors an innocent look when they fretted about those parts of their lawns not growing so well. When needed, she could activate the circle to keep her home safe from magical attacks. She didn't have to activate it very often, but Cary had always liked the "be prepared" aspect of Angie's circle. Not everyone had bosses who could arrange a protective glamour around one's house that kept interlopers from finding it.

If the witch was attacking, Angie would have her shield up. Although, she'd have had to drop it to let Cary, Lucy, and Marianne in. That could have opened a vulnerability. Cary wasn't feeling any of those tingles she got when someone was in need of her particular brand of magic, though. So she didn't think there was any immediate danger. But she couldn't be certain.

"She's not currently attacking," Angie said, confirming Cary's suspicion. "I just got a call, which I ignored because of my family being here. So she followed with a text. And then another text. And another. The tone is getting a little…intense."

"What does she want?" Lucy asked.

"For me to meet her in Forest Park."

"Well, we're not doing that," Cary said.

Angie frowned a little. "I'm afraid if I don't meet her, she'll come here. And I don't want my family in danger. All the kids are here." Both of Angie's brothers were married with multiple kids ranging in age from eleven to one year old. And Angie was a devoted aunt. "Only my oldest niece knows her Auntie is a real witch, and I don't want them forced to see things they aren't ready for. I don't want them going through what I did."

Cary narrowed her eyes at that. There were parts of Angie's past she never talked about. Things she sometimes—but rarely—referred to in oblique ways but never came out and explained. Occasionally, she said she would explain, but those conversations never seemed to happen. Cary tried not to push, despite her curiosity. People should be allowed their secrets. For example, her parents had no idea she was a magical Protector. They thought she did research for a professor she'd had in college who was now writing popular science books. And none of her friends knew about the glamour on her house. It was safer the fewer people who knew about it.

So people had secrets and that should be allowed, even when they were one of your best friends. And even if you really really wanted to ask them more.

"So we're going to the witch?" Marianne asked.

Angie glanced over her shoulder. "I don't want to leave them alone and unprotected."

"Two of us could stay here to keep them safe and the other one could go with you," Lucy said. "Divide and conquer."

"That could work." Angie continued to frown at her front door.

"Your parents will be okay with this?" Cary asked.

"They'll get it. Probably even approve if it means keeping this kind of chaos away from their grandkids."

Angie's mother was a witch too, but one with only a very minimal amount of power. Nothing like what Angie commanded. And she didn't have the added issue of also being psychic like Angie. The rest of Angie's family were perfectly ordinary, mundane humans. Even the nieces and nephews. According to Angie, this didn't diminish the chaos in her family even a little bit since kids were involved, but her father was good at handling chaos.

Angie gave Cary a look. "I'm torn."

"You want me to protect your family," Cary said. Because of course she'd want the Protector to stay here and keep her family safe. Cary would be loath to let Angie leave without her, but understood the priority here. Angie was capable of taking care of herself. Her family didn't have much, if any, defense against magical attacks. "I'll stay. So long as you promise to use your strongest shields and magic and stuff."

Angie flashed a quick smile. "Thanks. That'll help. And at least you've met my parents before." Cary had met them last year during one of their visits up from New Mexico.

"I'll stay here too," Lucy said. "You're going to need someone with magic at your back if you're facing a witch."

Lucy, while a multi-black belt holding martial artist who could kick the asses of men twice her side, even three times her size since she was pretty petite, she was the only one among their group of friends who didn't have any magic at all.

Marianne shrugged. "I've got your back. I'm sure I have some useful things in my purse to help with a rogue witch."

Marianne was a weaver. Outside of the usual—being able to weave straw into gold, which she considered little more than a parlor trick—she could also do some truly amazing things with thread and cloth. Her current purse was maybe the size of a shoebox on the outside, but that did not reflect the size of the interior. Cary had seen Marianne pull a full-sized spinning wheel out of a purse once. Her purses were never to be underestimated.

"Thanks," Angie said. "I appreciate the backup."

"We've got you," Marianne said.

"How much time do you have before this witch gets impatient?" Cary asked, heading up the steps to the porch.

She got a little tingling warning along her spine at the same time as a new voice said...

"No time at all."

3

"Well shit," Cary muttered. She hurried back down the steps and placed herself between the stranger and the rest of Angie's house, including her friends.

"What happened to Forest Park, Teresa?" Angie called. She didn't move away from her porch and her position blocking the front door.

Teresa was medium height, dark hair pulled up into a thick bun on top of her head, dark eyes narrowed as she took in Angie's house. Her age was hard to judge—and Cary was notoriously bad at figuring out people's ages—but at a guess, Cary would put her in her forties somewhere. She wore dark-wash jeans and a white, puffy winter coat. Outwardly, she was unassuming and ordinary looking. Nothing about her stood out as obviously "witchy". Which Cary had learned meant absolutely nothing when it came to witches.

Teresa smiled and shrugged. "I didn't think you'd actually come." She glanced at Marianne, Lucy, and Cary. "Reinforcements?"

"What do you want?" Angie asked without answering her question.

"You owe me. And I need your help."

"I don't owe you. We've discussed this. And I'm not helping you."

"It's not about the other thing," Teresa said. "This is…something different."

Oh, did Cary want to ask questions. So so many questions piling up just begging to spill out. She knew that would derail things. She knew it in her gut. But when most of your job was to just stand still and not let bad guys through, you filled the time by asking questions. She was a curious person anyway. And asking questions was a habit now.

She pressed her lips together to keep her mouth shut.

"Doesn't matter," Angie said. "I'm not helping you."

Teresa's gaze skimmed over Cary and the others again. "Why reinforcements?"

"Their friends," Angie said.

"Not witches." Teresa stared a Cary for a beat, her eyes narrowed. "Well, maybe you." She frowned. "Or maybe not. What are you?"

"Concerned citizen," Cary said. Her standard response to that question. A lot of people assumed she was a witch for some reason, sometimes even other witches. They couldn't read her or figure out what her magic was—and that was always better—but she'd never been sure why witch was the default assumption.

Teresa's dark eyes flared a little at Cary's response, as if it annoyed her, but she shifted her gaze back to Angie, dismissing Cary. Cary didn't take it personally.

"I saved your ass that one time," Teresa said.

"I'd beg to differ," Angie said. "As I recall, I saved my own ass. And yours as well."

"We could argue that point for the next few months. I need your help now." Teresa straightened her shoulders. "I'm asking, Angela. Please."

Angie cursed and let out a very loud sigh. "I'm not saying yes yet," she said, her deep voice a little deeper with her annoyance. "What's wrong?"

"I...I have a niece. She's been working with me."

Angie snarled loud enough for Cary to hear even though she was a few feet away. The sound actually made the hairs on Cary's arms rise. Wow. Whatever it meant that Teresa was working with her niece, it pissed Angie off.

"And she's missing," Teresa finished.

"Where?" Angie barked.

"Here. In Portland. That's why I got in touch with you."

Angie fell silent. Cary turned to look at her. She had her hands on her hips, her head tilted down as she shook it slowly back and forth, as if she'd deny Teresa's request for help. Whatever was between them, it was obviously bad. They weren't friends. And from Angie's reaction, she had a feeling Teresa had gotten her niece into whatever this trouble was in the first place.

But none of them could deny helping someone in trouble. It wasn't in their natures.

Cary hated to see Angie so torn, though. She opened her mouth, prepared to go get Teresa's niece so Angie didn't have to. Really, it was sort of her job description anyway. But before she could speak, Angie looked up, her green eyes hard as she stared at Teresa.

"Does this have anything, anything at all, to do with…" Angie paused, still glaring. "Anything to do with the work I don't do anymore?"

"No. We…went a different way this time. But she's missing, and you can scry."

Cary loved Angie. She respected her. And she would never want to force her to reveal something she wasn't prepared to reveal. But… So. Many. Questions.

"I can go," Cary said. "If you find her, I'll go get her." She glanced at Teresa. "That's kind of what I do."

"That doesn't tell me what you are?" Teresa pointed out.

"Nope. It doesn't."

"This is my problem, Cary," Angie said. "Not yours. Not your job."

"Well, I mean, it sort of is. Sounds like a good guy…?" She asked that rather than said it because she wasn't honestly sure what category to put Teresa and her niece in. Angie shrugged. Okay, so… "Teresa's niece is in trouble. And I get between trouble and people all the time. That is the very definition of my job."

"We'll all help," Lucy said.

"Sounds like you might need a little backup," Marianne said. "We're stronger together, the four of us."

Angie's glare softened as she looked at them. "You three really are the best." Her glare returned when she looked at Teresa. "If I allow my friends to put themselves in danger to help me, you have to let me touch you first."

Angie was a touch psychic. She touched things and read them. Sometimes future. Sometimes past. Sometimes she saw what was happening in that moment. It depended on the object and its history. She had a great deal of control over her skill—she wouldn't be able to touch anything in the world if she didn't—so she rarely read anything or anyone by accident. It happened. But, according to Angie, not often these days.

If she was asking to touch Teresa, she was asking to read her. And from the flare of Teresa's nostrils and the way her mouth flattened, Teresa knew exactly what Angie was asking.

"You aren't going to like some of what you see," Teresa said.

Angie snorted. "That isn't surprising."

"Will you scry for her?"

"Probably. At the very least. If I confirm you haven't been messing in realms you shouldn't, I'll probably even help you get her back. But I'm not leaving this house if you refuse to let me read you."

"How's your aura reading now?"

"Excellent. Thanks. That's not what I mean."

"Been practicing a lot, have you?"

"You're avoiding my request. That won't help your niece."

Teresa let out a string of Spanish that Cary assumed was cursing based on the one or two Spanish curse words she knew. She sucked at languages in general, so she had no idea what Teresa was saying. But those two words and her tone made it pretty obvious she wasn't saying nice complimentary things.

"Fine," Teresa snapped. She held out a hand, scowling at Angie. "But don't say I didn't warn you."

4

Angie came off her porch, with Marianne and Lucy at her back, and Cary taking the lead as they all approached Teresa. Teresa rolled her eyes at them as she continued to hold her hand out for Angie.

"You don't need the phalanx," Teresa said. "I need your help. I'm not here to cause trouble."

"Do you know," Cary said conversationally as they stopped right in front of the witch, close enough Angie could touch her while Cary was still between them, "I have heard that before. From bad guys. And my friend doesn't trust you, so we won't."

Teresa's scowl softened into an almost smile. Not quite, but her mouth did tilt up a little at the sides. "You always could pick 'em," she said to Angie.

"You ready?" Angie ignored all the banter.

Teresa lifted her hand a little more.

Angie stared at the woman's palm for a long moment before settling her hand over Teresa's in a gentle touch. She closed her eyes.

When she snapped them open, she snarled at Teresa again. "Later, when there's no one else around, we are going to have words," she said.

"Later. I need to get my niece back."

"Right." Angie released her hand and gave her a nod. "What did you bring me?"

For a beat, Cary had no idea what Angie was talking about. Then Teresa pulled a glove from her pocket and handed it to Angie. And Cary remembered Angie would need a personal item to scry for Teresa's niece.

The glove was a thick, red faux-leather with a simple stitched pattern on the back. Angie took the glove and closed her eyes for a moment. She hissed a quiet curse, opened her eyes, and shook her head at Teresa.

"Find her first, judge us later," Teresa said.

Angie turned back toward her house. "Give me a minute."

Cary followed Angie, and Teresa followed Cary. Teresa made it half way up the walk before coming to a stop. She frowned a little and looked around, pressing at the air.

"You put up a shield?" she asked Angie.

"House is full of people," Angie said. "That's as close as you get."

Cary held her position in between Teresa and the house. She was pretty sure it was her Protector magic keeping Teresa back and not anything Angie had conjured. For one thing, Angie hadn't done any of the usual hand gestures and quiet murmured words that triggered her spells. But also, Cary heard Angie's "saying a thing without saying it" in her tone—they'd worked together often enough at this stage that she could tell when what Angie said had a double meaning.

In this case, Cary took her words as a reminder to Cary that the house was full of vulnerable people, people a Protector would need to keep safe.

Whatever else Angie was willing to do here, she definitely had Teresa in the "bad guy" category. And apparently, so did Cary's Protector magic since it was holding Teresa back. Her curiosity about what Teresa had done to earn her bad guy status was hard to contain, though.

Angie went inside her house. From the open door, Cary heard her talking to someone, too quietly for the words to be clear, but she thought she heard "okay" and "work." Since her brothers and her parents knew what Angie's work was, she hoped they'd keep everyone inside and safe and not try to ride out to the rescue. People had to let Cary protect them for her to keep them safe.

As they waited, Cary, Marianne, and Lucy all stared at Teresa. Teresa stared back, her mouth quirked in a "you don't intimidate me" look. Which just went to show she had no idea what she was facing. Lucy alone should have caused her to cower. She'd have her mind blown if she saw what Marianne could pull out of her purse.

Cary had some pretty amazing friends.

She considered Teresa for a long moment before finally giving in to curiosity. "While we wait, want to bad guy monologue and tell us all what's happening?"

"My niece is missing," Teresa said. "Missed that part?"

Cary snorted. "Do you know who took her?"

"Yes."

"Do you know why?"

"Yes."

"That's the explanation I'd love to hear then. Why would someone kidnap your niece?"

"I'm not in the mood to tell that story."

Cary sighed. She sort of assumed that. Still, never hurt to try. "Any stories you might want to tell? Maybe about the bad guy who kidnapped her? I mean, there's no reason you can't bad guy monologue about another bad guy, right?"

"He is a bad person," Teresa said with a snarl. "Evil. And he deserves everything he gets."

"Fair enough. What's he done?"

"Cheats, lies, steals from the hungry. He hoards and leaves others suffering. He thinks he's above the law."

Cary nodded. "Sounds like an asshole."

"He is."

"Asshole doesn't necessarily equal evil. For example, I can be a real asshole, but I'm not evil."

The comment must have startled Teresa because she barked out a laugh and then frowned and blinked at her own reaction.

Cary wagged her eyebrows in acknowledgment of Teresa's unintended amusement. Then she said, "That part about stealing from the hungry doesn't sound good, though."

"He starts charities, claiming he'll give the money to the poor and hungry. He even cons some of the organizations he's claiming to help into endorsing his efforts and making him look legitimate. Then he pockets almost all the money through loopholes and corporate speak and leaves those desperate people with crumbs."

"That does sound like a dick move," Lucy said.

"I take it the authorities have been no help with convicting him of fraud?" Marianne said. She sounded particularly angry about the man's scam.

"They've let the rich white man go multiple times," Teresa said.

"Of course they did," Marianne said, her voice clipped and sharp.

Cary glanced back at her and mouthed, "You okay?"

Marianne nodded, but she was frowning fiercely.

That didn't bode well for the asshole stealing money from charities for the hungry. Not that Cary cared. She wasn't feeling any warm and fuzzy feelings for this particular asshole anyway.

She faced Teresa again. "What are *you* doing about this particular con artist that got your niece kidnapped and has Angie upset?"

Teresa glanced at the house. "She can tell you why she's upset. What I've done… Nothing he doesn't deserve. Nothing he doesn't bring on himself. If he didn't ask for these things, he wouldn't be in this position to begin with."

"Spells and such?"

Since Teresa was a witch, Cary had to assume this was something to do with curses. Angie hated curses. She was very careful about the kinds of spells she used. The most punishing spell Cary had ever witnessed her use against another witch was a bounce back spell— basically whatever the witch sent out, she got back. Since that particular witch had been doing very bad things, what she got back was…not pretty.

But if that's all Teresa had done, Angie wouldn't be so angry with her. No, Teresa had done something much worse than just toss the man's actions back on himself. Bad enough she was in the "bad guy" category for Cary's magic. Cary didn't control her magic, it just worked when it needed to, when good guys needed protecting. Her magic was working to keep Teresa from the house. Whatever else, the woman was a threat here. Even if her story made her look like a good guy out for justice.

Cary had learned over the last few years as a Protector that sometimes bad guys were complicated—including their status as "bad."

Which was why she was frequently glad her powers just worked. Not having control of them could, at times, suck. But since they seemed to have more of an awareness of who was and who wasn't a threat than she did, it was nice they self-directed at those moments.

"And such," Teresa answered Cary's question.

Without actually answering it, Cary noticed. But since she did the same thing to people all the time she felt a little hypocritical for her annoyance. That didn't stop her wanting to push for more answers. She just acknowledged she was being hypocritical about it.

Angie had left the door cracked open, not enough for Teresa to see in, but just enough Cary could hear movement from inside, quiet conversation, and then Angie reemerged onto the porch.

"Everything okay?" Cary asked keeping most of her attention on Teresa.

"Fine. My oldest brother is going to keep everyone entertained while we're gone."

"You found her?" Teresa asked.

Cary took Angie's grunt as an affirmative.

"You still want us all to come with you?" Lucy asked Angie quietly. "Seems like it might be good to have friends on hand that have your back."

"This will be easier with fewer people," Teresa said. "Just you."

"Well in that case," Cary said, "of course we're going with you two. You still fall into the bad guy category, and I'm not letting you walk my friend into a trap."

"Me neither," Marianne said.

"I'm with you," Lucy echoed.

"You can do that thing once we head off?" Cary asked Angie, glancing back at her. She'd put on shoes—hiking boots—and a gray puffer coat over her sweater.

"I can," Angie said.

Cary was glad she'd picked up the reference to the protective circle. Cary didn't like to talk about things out loud in front of bad guys if she could help it because discretion always seemed like a better idea than blabbing about protective spells and things. The less the bad guys knew about your defenses, the better in her experience.

"Were are we going?" Marianne asked.

"Scrying indicates a place near Bridlemile," Angie said. "Southwest part of the city." She gave an address in a neighborhood with some of the most expensive house prices in the city.

"He'd be in a comfortable house," Teresa said. "That makes sense."

"What did he ask from you in return for your niece?" Angie asked. "He kidnapped her, didn't kill her."

Yet, Cary thought but didn't say out loud.

"What did he ask you for in exchange for her life?" Angie said.

"Nothing I'm prepared to give. I want my niece back. I'm not bargaining for her. He won't stick to any bargains anyway. He'll cheat or find a loophole, like he's used to doing. I'm not letting him get away with that with my niece's life on the line."

"Maybe you shouldn't have involved her in the first place," Angie said. Her voice was still hard as diamond, sharp and ready to cut.

"That's not your business. Help me get her back and I'll go away again. Without bringing your past into your cozy new life."

A beat of silence, then, "You don't have any part of my past to bring into my cozy new life. You don't know what you think you know."

"I know enough."

Another beat of silence. Cary risked a glance at Angie. Her expression had gone blank, impossible to read. She'd never seen Angie look that way before. She'd seen her angry, scared, annoyed, accepting, all manner of emotions. But not blank. Not so entirely unreadable.

Whatever the hell was in Angie's past that linked her with this witch, it was something she didn't want talked about even a little.

"We'll meet you there," Angie said finally. "Don't do anything until we arrive. I didn't get a good picture of what's happening or what could be happening. I just saw the location."

There was no emotion in her tone. Or maybe there was, a lot of it, but all suppressed so that it came out sounding emotionless. Like all the colors of visible light all getting mashed together until the only color visible was white.

Teresa glanced at all of them in turn, her gaze settling for an extended moment on Cary. "You're definitely coming with her."

"I am," Cary said.

Teresa nodded, her opinion on the matter carefully hidden.

Cary didn't really care one way or the other how Teresa felt about her presence in all this. She intended to have Angie's back. Or, rather, her front because that's where Cary had to stand to protect her. But the sentiment was the same. They all had Angie's back.

She wasn't going into this without them.

5

As soon as Teresa got into her car and drove away, Angie's shoulders relaxed and she let out a very emphatic, but quiet, curse.

"I feel that," Marianne said. "You okay?"

"No. Let's get this done. I don't like having her in my city."

"What she said…" Marianne started, hesitating around her words, as if not sure how to say what she needed to say. "What she said about the man behind the kidnapping…?"

"That he's a horrible person who deserves what he gets? I'm sure he is."

"How did you know that's what she told us?" Lucy asked.

"That's who she hunts," Angie said. "Teresa goes after powerful people who think they're above the law and uses that against them to punish them."

"That doesn't sound like a bad thing to me," Marianne said.

"It wouldn't be if she didn't so often put innocent people in danger without any regard to the consequences for those innocents," Angie said. "If she didn't use…means that shouldn't be dabbled in. Not even for revenge. She unleashes things best left leashed in her quest. And more often than not, the results are worse than the original crimes of her victims. The collateral damage is too high. I have no sympathy for the people she goes after. Not even a little bit. But her methods leave a lot to be desired."

Marianne nodded, her lips pursed as she stared at the place where Teresa's car had been.

Cary studied her friends. "We okay with this? Maybe Lucy and Marianne want to stay here?" she asked because Marianne's thoughtful expression struck her as…complicated. And maybe none of them wanted to complicate this situation any more than it was.

Marianne blinked and refocused on them all. "I'm good. I don't like vigilantes, if that's what you all are worried about. I understand the desire." She shrugged. "Maybe a little too well. But I've also seen how that need can get twisted into an evil of its own. Teresa's crossed that line. It's in her eyes."

"My powers were working," Cary said quietly, too quietly for anyone outside her friends to hear.

Marianne nodded. "Crossed the line," she repeated.

They all knew what it meant that Cary's powers worked against Teresa. She was a threat. To Angie, to Angie's family, to Marianne and Lucy… It didn't really matter. Cary had been protecting the people behind her from Teresa. Which made Teresa someone they couldn't trust.

"Let's take one car," Lucy said. "We want to arrive together."

"Mine," Marianne said. She had the largest and most comfortable car.

"On the drive, I'll tell you what I didn't tell Teresa," Angie said, following Marianne to her BMW.

"You saw more while scrying," Cary guessed.

"And when I touched her niece's glove."

THEY PARKED A FEW BLOCKS FROM THEIR DESTINATION, NEAR A luxurious-looking retirement home, so they could walk to the house, keeping a low profile. The afternoon was bright and sunny but some darker clouds were rolling in from the horizon, bringing rain and dampness to the cold air.

The neighborhood Angie's scrying had led them to was a nice, lush place. Lots of greenery, tall trees, carefully maintained yards. The houses were on the larger side, and spaced with plenty of land around them, but not quite mansions. Some of them were close, though.

Given what Teresa had said about her niece's kidnapper, Cary thought he might be wealthy. The neighborhood was definitely nice, and well beyond her current means, but it didn't strike her as the place a wealthy con artist might live since these weren't actual mansions. Then again, what did she know about wealthy con artists. The closest she got to mega wealth were vampires, and she tried very hard not to get too close to them. Outside of that one incident. But drinking blood from kittens should never be tolerated. It was just wrong.

"So," Lucy said as Marianne locked up her car, "we have a woman who's been using blood and sacrifice magic to destroy the life of a man who's been using his money and connections to destroy the world. Did I get that right?"

"None of it sounded good," Marianne said.

"To be honest, it's not the worst thing I've seen Teresa use," Angie said quietly. "But it's getting close. The sacrifices have all been animals. So far. But I don't put it past her to move up to more powerful sacrifices."

"And the magic she's conjuring, all of it is directed at this particular bad guy?" Cary asked.

"Right now. Yes. They've been…torturing him with sickness and aging spells. Apparently, he's terrified of aging, of looking old. And he's a germaphobe who can't tolerate being ill."

"That's…" Marianne trailed off.

"Say it," Angie encouraged. Her voice was deep but she didn't sound angry, just resigned.

"That doesn't sound so bad. Like the sort of thing a man who steals money from charities deserves," Marianne finished with a shrug. "Not even as bad as what my sisters and I had to do to the goblin king."

Cary tried not to shudder. It had been a couple of years since that happened. The goblin king had forced Marianne and her sisters' hands, but none of them had viewed the outcome as...pleasant.

"Right up until the end," Angie said, "the goblin king had a choice to refuse what you offered. This isn't an act-right-or-you-die sort of thing. And Teresa's methods aren't..." Angie let out a breath. "She won't stop with just a little light spellcasting to make him suffer some of his fears. She'll move up to human sacrifice to make this one man suffer."

"Doesn't that sort of...defeat the purpose of what she's doing?" Lucy asked.

"She'll choose another person she deems 'deserving of death' to use for the sacrifice and call it justified." Angie shook her head. "Teresa's need for vengeance on people like this con artist pushes her into deals with devils and evil acts to punish other evil doers. She doesn't see the hypocrisy in it."

"Crossed a line," Marianne murmured again. Quietly, though, as if she were speaking to herself.

"We rescue the niece," Cary said. "But...do we rescue the con artist? Or... How is this going to work? None of them seem like, well, good guys here."

She always had trouble with the muddy middle of these sorts of situations. Usually, she had her faery mentor Jaxer around to advise her, to let her know what she was supposed to do when the situation seemed too complex to sort out herself. This time around, no such luck. The only certainty she had was that she would keep Angie, Marianne, and Lucy safe no matter what else happened.

And maybe that was her only job here.

They found Teresa waiting for them just around the corner from their destination, leaning against her black SUV—a rental from what Cary could tell.

"Tell them everything?" Teresa asked, smirking.

"Enough," Angie said without rising to the bait implied in the smirk.

"Not everything then." Teresa sounded smug.

"Cary and Marianne are big time animal lovers," Angie said,

almost as if changing the subject. "I didn't want them trying to kill you before we made sure your niece was safe."

Cary looked at Marianne, who looked back at her, then they both frowned at Teresa. Angie had mentioned the blood magic was fueled by animal sacrifice, but she hadn't been specific. Cary had read enough to make some assumptions about what that sacrifice had entailed. And her assumptions had led her to a quick and fast knife slice across the neck of a goat or a fast hatchet to a chicken's neck. She didn't like either of those visuals, but the deaths of animals sacrificed in blood magic were *normally* quick. She hated it, and liked Teresa even less for using that kind of magic, but given Angie's comment, and the implied information she'd left out, Cary was starting to hate Teresa.

"Definitely not a good guy," Cary muttered.

"No," Marianne said.

"It'll be interesting to find out what other pertinent information you haven't told them," Teresa said, her smug tone dropping.

"Stop threatening me, or I leave," Angie said. She held Teresa's gaze. She hadn't raised her voice at all. In fact, she'd gone quieter and her voice had deepened again. But she didn't do anything overtly aggressive to the other witch. Just held her gaze.

Whatever Teresa saw there, she lowered her gaze first and said, "Let's get this done. I'm worried about Ava."

Huh. That was…interesting. Cary wasn't sure what the exchange meant, but she filed it away.

They rounded the bend and walked to the house from Angie's scrying in silence. The roads were empty, not even any people out walking dogs. Cary's neighborhood was quiet during the day but that was because everyone on the street had jobs. Except for the retired couple a few doors down, no one was home in the middle of the afternoon. And the retired couple spent a lot of time traveling. But this had struck Cary as the kind of neighborhood where a lot of people didn't have to work anymore. Maybe she'd been wrong about it.

Or maybe some human instinct for trouble was keeping the place clear.

Or maybe they were just having a stroke of good luck.

Cary's life hadn't entailed a lot of that kind of thing while working lately, though, so she had a hard time believing the empty street was just luck.

The house Angie led them to fit perfectly into the neighborhood. Two, maybe three stories if the attic had been converted, and made of large gray bricks that didn't seem very practical in an area that occasionally got earthquakes. The place was large and elevated from the sidewalk by a hilly, grass-covered yard. The double doors were elaborately carved wood and covered by a wrought iron gate with a large and obvious lock that seemed a little…excessive for ordinary home protection. The windows were also covered by wrought iron gates, both bottom floor and top. But the wrought iron was decoratively curved and added rather than detracted from the house's overall grandeur.

Fancy lights stood along the stone steps that led up through the yard to the front door, reminding Cary of old fashioned gaslamps. Though they weren't on at the moment, she imagined they were a nice bit of extra light at night. The stone stairs were a little steep and narrow and would probably be pretty slick in the rain.

"So," she murmured. "Do we…knock?"

"Sure," Angie said. "Let's see what we have to work with."

Teresa scowled at them. "Knock? Just walk up to the door and knock?"

"Or ring the bell," Angie said without looking at her—she was focused on the house. "Whatever gets their attention."

Without a word, Cary took the lead up the steps to the front door, Angie just behind her followed by Teresa. Marianne and Lucy took up the rear. The area in front of the door was narrow enough that Marianne and Lucy were left standing on the steps.

Cary knocked and ensured she was standing between the door and her companions. She heard Angie murmuring something quietly under her breath. She didn't dare ask what spell she was initiating, but whatever it was, Cary trusted her. And intended to cover her so she had time to cast the spell.

The problem, sometimes, with a witch's magic was that most of it took time. Very few things could be done instantaneously unless the witch had some sort of pre-prepared vial of potion or warded object to work with. Wizards had instant weapons they could call on—fire balls, energy bolts, that kind of thing—but witch magic took the time it took.

Normally, under non-dangerous situations, this didn't matter. In dangerous, potentially changeable situations, the unprepared witch could get into trouble.

Fortunately, Angie might as well have been a girl scout because she was almost always prepared.

And she had a shield keeping her safe in the meantime.

Her own personal walking, talking Kevlar vest.

Cary smiled at the man who opened the door. "Hello," she said. "We're here to collect…Ava?" She turned to check the name with Teresa. Teresa frowned but nodded. Cary faced the man again. "Ava."

The man's gaze traveled over their group before settling on Teresa. Ignoring Cary completely, he said, "Did you bring what I told you to bring?"

"Right in front of you," she said. "This is the demon witch. Now give me back my niece."

Cary scowled.

Well, that didn't sound good.

6

The man standing in the doorway started to smile. The look was not pleasant. He wasn't particularly tall, but not short either. An inch maybe two taller than Cary, probably not even quite as tall as Angie. He had ordinary brown hair in a neat short cut, hazel eyes that might have been attractive on someone else, and a narrow jaw that gave him a pointy look. His features individually weren't bad or anything, but the combination was a little…off-putting. Cary wasn't sure how to describe it. Not bad. But not welcoming either.

If this was the con artist, how the hell did people look at him and think, "This is a guy I can trust," because Cary wanted to take a few steps away from him and ensure he didn't touch her. It was pure instinct, though. There wasn't anything about him that should have had her hackles up.

Well, apart from that slimy, eager smile.

He took a step out of the front door, his gaze zeroed in on Angie. But he came up short against Cary's shield and scowled.

"What's going on?" he barked, looking between Angie and Teresa. "You said she wouldn't be shielded."

"You said you'd let Ava go after I brought her here," Teresa said. "We all lied. But I am getting my niece back. Now."

"What the hell is a demon witch, by the way?" Cary asked, just to throw the scowling man off his game and give Angie more time to do whatever it was she was doing. Cary noticed Teresa hadn't moved forward, hadn't tried to get around her yet. Teresa didn't know what kind of shield Cary had, but she wasn't in a hurry to get out from behind it with this man.

"You can't have her until I get what I want," the man said to Teresa, still ignoring Cary. "That was the deal. And no shield will stop that."

"I beg to differ," Cary said.

He continued to ignore her. "You made this deal. I expect you to live up to it. All it'll take is a single word and your niece is dead."

"You kill her, I'll have no reason not to slaughter you," Teresa said. "If I were you, I wouldn't be in a hurry to bring that on. I won't kill you quickly."

Cary had to suppress a shiver at the hate in Teresa's voice. She wouldn't want to be on the bad side of this woman's killing rage.

"No one is killing anyone," she said, still trying to get the man to focus on her. She was the shield here, and being distracted by her gave the others—gave Angie—time to work. "You never answered my question."

"If you don't know, you don't need to know," the man said, looking down his nose at Cary like she was beneath his interest. Given he wasn't all that much taller than her, the effect of him attempting to look "down" at her was a little comical. Seriously, did people *really* believe this guy gave money to charities?

"Not seeing it," she said, mostly to herself.

"Not… What?" he said.

She grinned. Now she had him. "You. I mean. You're obviously a thief and a conman. It's like…right there in your face. How on earth can you con people when you're that obviously crooked? You should work on that, try to fix your expressions or something. Not that I want you to keep bilking charities or anything, but it must be really hard to do your job when the sliminess oozes off of you so strongly."

From behind her, she heard Lucy's high, sweet, snort of amusement.

The man's scowl turned fierce.

"We should probably go inside," Cary said. "Get Ava." She took a step forward. Mostly, she was just pressing buttons to keep the man's attention on her, but when she stepped forward, he stumbled backward a few steps.

Huh. That was interesting.

To Angie, who'd stopped murmuring just as Cary made to move inside, she said, "Shall we?"

"Sure," Angie said. "Wouldn't mind getting a look at the place."

"Fair enough." Cary took another step forward and the man stumbled backward again, her shield pushing him out of the way. Well, that was useful.

"You want us to cover out here or come in with you?" Marianne asked.

That was a real tricky question. Cary didn't want to leave them outside her protection. No one could just sneak up on her anyway, so so long as she had everyone within her shield, they were all safe. But having eyes on the sidewalk in case the con artist had accomplices, as he'd implied, and those accomplices tried to sneak Ava out of the house seemed like a good idea.

She looked back at Marianne and Lucy, eyes narrowed.

"We got this," Marianne assured. "We'll just…keep an eye on things." She had her hand in her purse. Which meant she had something in there that would help in this situation. It could be anything from a taser gun to an entire arsenal of weapons. To some magical cloth that smothered bad guys. The contents of Marianne's purses were always interesting.

"We're good," Lucy said. She was carefully balanced, her stance wide. And because she was still in her gi, she reminded Cary of how she looked at the front of a class full of students she was about to run through a particularly hard workout. Or she was about to toss Cary around the dojo in an attempt to improve Cary's extremely lacking self-defense skills.

"Call if you need us," Cary said firmly. "Or if…you see anything."

Lucy shifted to scanning the street as Marianne did a slow circle, her hand still inside her purse.

Teresa moved in closer to Cary and Angie, but, Cary noticed, she didn't seem able to get very close to Angie and scowled a little when she was forced by Cary's shield to stop.

So. Definitely still a threat, especially to Angie. Cary wasn't keen on having her at their backs, and having her between Cary and Marianne and Lucy. But they were here for Teresa's niece so she supposed they had to let Teresa come inside with them. Still, Cary was glad her shield was protecting Angie from the other witch.

She faced forward again and stepped into the house. The con artist had been trying to push at her shield, she realized, trying to physically force her back outside. She shook her head at him.

"That's not how this works," she told him and moved into the house further.

He stumbled away so awkwardly he nearly landed on his ass.

"Watch your step," Cary said in a pleasant tone of voice just to irritate him.

"You are not invited in here," the man snarled.

"I'm not a vampire. I don't need an invitation." She pushed a little farther forward. "Though I have to admit that is a really cool bit of insurance for us poor mortals."

"What?"

"That you have to *invite* a vampire inside, or they can't enter your home. It's nice really, because, frankly, the bastards are scary dangerous. I try not to deal with them any more often than I have to. So far, that's been minimal. Except for that time with the kitten-sucking vampire. But really, he should not have been drinking from kittens. I mean, who does that? It's just sick on so many levels."

During her rambling she managed to push the con artist several feet into the house, far enough to get a pretty good view of the interior.

Not bad. Not to her taste. But not as bad as she'd been expecting. She wasn't sure why she was anticipating lots of gold and gilt and gaudy ostentatiousness. This guy seemed that type.

Instead, the interior was laid out in dark, wood-paneled walls, inlaid, polished floors, dark wall hangings and even darker rugs. There was an overhead light which was turned off, the windows along the front of the house had their curtains closed so no one would see inside, and there didn't seem to be any more light coming from the back of the house. Which made the place, with all its dark décor, feel very gloomy. Kind of oppressive. Or maybe that was the thick hit of some sort of cologne that...well, it sort of smelled like someone had spilled a bottle of it and hadn't bothered to air the place out. And it wasn't one of those nice smelling colognes either. Lots of alcohol in the base of this one that made her nose twitch.

"Uh..." She lifted her hand and rocked it back and forth. "Yeah, I suppose the place is okay. Not something I'd have done, but you know, to each their own."

The con artist hadn't stopped blinking at her since she went on her vampire ramble.

"Are you...okay?" he asked her. "Like, in your head?"

She barked out a laugh. "You kidnapped a witch in order to con her witch aunt into bringing you another witch, and you're asking if *I'm okay*? I'm not the one who's risked the wrath of some seriously powerful magic wielders, bub." She'd risked the wrath of other seriously powerful beings in the last few years, but he didn't need to know that. "You got a name? Or are you just Con Artist? For the record."

"I'm not giving my name to witches and a woman who's crazy enough to believe in vampires."

She raised her brows at him. "You're okay with witch magic but think vampires are a supernatural step too far? Wow. Sheltered." She tisked. "Why did you think you could forbid my entering your house with the whole 'not invited' nonsense, then?"

"I...I didn't invite you in."

"My man, I think you might be in over your head here." She sighed and turned to Angie. "Got a bead on our kidnapped niece."

"I'm thinking back of the house." She reached out and touched the door behind her, the door knob which Con Artist had so recently been holding.

Cary rocked back on her heals, hands in the pockets of her leather coat, and smiled at Con Artist when he tried to rush them. He charged with his head lowered as if he intended to tackle her or something. She just shook her head when he hit against her shield, hard, and stumbled backward, rubbing his head.

"Huh," Angie murmured.

"Get something?" Cary asked.

"Yeah. She's on the second floor. He's got two accomplices—at least two that have touched this door." She looked at Con Artist again. "And he's got some pretty dangerous folks looking to kill him because he went one con too far with the wrong people."

"Figures. He seems like that sort of guy." She tisked at him again.

"Shut the fuck up," he hissed.

"Language," Cary said primly. She wasn't one to talk. She cussed all the time. But she figured it would piss him off, so she was happy to be hypocritical in this instant.

"Let's get my niece," Teresa said. "His mob troubles are his own making."

"Are they?" Angie asked her, her head tilted to one side. "Or did you, perhaps, help that along?"

"Nothing he wasn't already going to do," Teresa said with a shrug.

"You—" Angie cut herself off and pressed her lips together. She shook her head. "Let's get Ava." She gestured to the stairs near the back of the hallway. They were simple dark wood, covered by a dark blue runner.

Cary straightened and headed toward the stairs.

"This isn't our deal," the man roared.

"Do you know his name?" Cary asked Teresa, giving some of his own back to him by ignoring him.

"Not his real name," Teresa said. "He uses a lot of false names in his…line of work."

"His name is Ken," Angie said matter-of-factly. "Ken Kowalski. From Pennsylvania."

"Nice to meet you, Ken," Cary said. "Well, okay, not really. But at least I can call you something other than Con Artist."

"How…how the hell did you know my name?" Ken said, stumbling against the staircase, still trying to keep them from moving farther into the house.

"I'm a witch," Angie said with a shrug. She didn't elaborate. She was as good at being vague about her skills as Cary was.

"She's a touch psychic," Teresa said with an eye roll.

So much for remaining vague about Angie's skills. Cary gave Teresa a scowl. The woman smirked back.

Cary's turn to roll her eyes.

"I…" Ken stuttered. "She's supposed to, to call…" He looked between Teresa and Angie. "She's not the one, is she?" he snapped. "You just brought some random witch, not the one you promised."

"No, she's the one," Teresa said with a shrug. "Just not her only skill."

"You know what they're talking about?" Cary asked Angie with a frown.

"Yup."

"You gonna tell me about it?"

"Maybe one day. The stuff I can tell you. But not today. The less discussed today, in front of Ken here, the better."

Teresa opened her mouth, but Angie made a hand gesture and the other witch seemed to freeze with her mouth open. Teresa's eyes widened, but she didn't otherwise move.

"What'd you do to her?" Cary asked, not really concerned but definitely curious. She hadn't seen Angie do that before.

"Little stall spell. She isn't hurt."

"Wasn't worried," Cary assured. "Stall spell? Freezes her in place?"

"Delays and slows her down so much, she's essentially frozen."

"Cool. That what you were working on outside?"

"One of the things," Angie said.

Even better. "Shall we get Ava so we can get out of here? Feels like this is a trap, and we're in the middle of it."

"It is," Angie said with a nod. "And we are."

"All right, then." Cary faced the erstwhile Ken Kowalski who was still trying to push her away from the stairs. "Up we go."

7

The upstairs continued the decorative tastes of the first floor. Lots of dark wood and deep, jewel-toned rugs, not nearly enough light, a gloomy feeling over the whole place punctuated by that stench of spilled cologne.

Teresa stomped up the stairs a moment behind them, no longer frozen by Angie's spell. She glared at Angie and opened her mouth to say something. Angie raised her brows and her hand at the same time. Teresa—wisely to Cary's way of thinking—kept her mouth shut. Though she didn't stop scowling. And Cary was pretty sure she didn't like that look in Teresa's eyes.

The landing on the second floor had a railing that reminded Cary of one of those horror movies where someone inevitably fell over the railing to their death. She didn't watch a lot of horror films—too much like a busman's holiday; she preferred action films and superhero movies, which could technically also count as busman's holiday, but screw it, they were her favorites—but she'd seen enough to know that that railing didn't bode well for someone. She arranged herself to stay between Angie and the bad guy but also so she was between her friend and the railing.

She was less concerned with Teresa since Teresa had betrayed Angie to get her here.

Not that Teresa was a friend or a good person or anything. But usually that didn't stop Cary from begrudgingly protecting someone that needed it. She hated protecting bad guys, but sometimes it couldn't be helped.

Usually, though, those bad guys hadn't just tried to use her best friend as a bargaining chip.

She gave Angie a look, then nodded each direction on the landing. There were two ways to go, and closed doors lined the halls on either side. The left was short, a few feet of hallway and only two doors. The right was a longer corridor with three different doors that Cary could see. But that corridor seemed to bend a little toward the back of the house, looking like maybe there was another room around that bend. Windows at each end of the corridors cast what little light there was on the second floor.

Angie considered the two directions, then raised her brows at Teresa, before pointing to the right, longer corridor. "Got the impression she was that way. There are two other people in this house. We'll have to get her from them."

Ken the Con Artist had backed into that right corridor, but his narrowed gaze jumped to the left corridor. And his panicked denial, his attempts to stop or slow them down despite Cary's shield, turned into a smirk.

Wow. He was really bad at this. How in the absolute hell had he conned people? It was all just *right there on his face*.

He'd do to learn some things from Angie. She was much better at playing this game.

"You lead," Teresa said to her. "No tricks with Ava's life."

Cary snorted. "You're the one to talk about no tricks."

Teresa and Angie both ignored the comment.

"We'll get her," Angie said. "Safe and sound."

"Not before I get what I want," Ken spat.

"What do you want?" Cary asked, curious. Not that she intended to let him get what he wanted. Unless he wanted to go to jail for fraud and kidnapping. She'd be okay with arranging to give him that.

"I need help. With the mob. I need… If I can make a deal with the right sort of demon, I can get out of this mess *and* get everything I want. I just need the right demon."

Cary narrowed her eyes, glanced at Angie, glanced back at Ken. "You wanted a witch brought to you to help you summon a demon?"

Ken grunted, which wasn't really an answer.

"First, always a bad idea making a deal with a demon. They *will* find the loopholes." Or so she'd read.

She tried to avoid dealing with demons as much as she tried to avoid vampires. She didn't seem to have very good luck with avoiding demons, though. She'd had to deal with a couple over the years. And that damned demon who'd kicked a puppy was the reason she'd gotten tricked into this job. So she'd read quite a lot about them. And the one very very important thing she'd learned was that they *always* found the loophole in the bargains they made with humans. All. Ways.

Which was why calling one on purpose always struck her as a monumentally stupid thing to do.

"Second," she continued because Ken started to speak to the whole loopholes issue and she wasn't ready for him to speak yet, "why do you need a witch? If you're stupid enough to summon a demon, you can do that on your own. And then face the demon hunters when they arrive to save your sorry ass. If they arrive in time." She shrugged. She didn't know a lot about demon hunters personally. She hadn't met one yet. But she got the impression there were only so many to go around. Bit like Protectors in that way.

"Third, and I can't emphasize this enough," she said, again before Ken could speak, "making a deal with a demon is a really really stupid idea."

"You said that twice," Ken said, snarling.

"It bears repeating," Cary said. "But let's get to the 'why you need a witch for this' part." She pushed forward toward the right corridor, her shield forcing Ken back several steps.

He stumbled and cursed at her, but he was no longer trying to push back and keep her from making progress. She wanted to shake her head at him, but she let it go.

"I don't need just any witch," he said, some of the earlier haughty smugness creeping back into his voice. "I need *her*." He pointed at Angie.

"Nope," Angie said.

"You heard her," Cary said. "She's not helping you." Cary wasn't even sure what Angie could do for the man. But that was something she'd ask Angie about later.

"That's what she thinks," Ken said, his lips lifting in an evil smile.

Cary was pretty sure she'd have been worried if Ken wasn't so supremely bad at all this.

The scream from behind them didn't even make her flinch.

She did turn around to see some sort of lightshow going on just behind Teresa, who had jumped closer to Cary. That move kind of surprised Cary. She'd been certain Teresa knew which direction the trap was going to come from. Maybe not. Or maybe she was just trying to avoid the cloud of...

Whatever the hell that was hanging in the air just beyond her shield.

8

____

The magical spell hovering in the air outside of her shield sort of reminded Cary of the stuff that came out of fire extinguishers. But purple. And a little more sparkly. Thicker than fog, with a grainy sand like texture, but not as thick as mud. Dense enough she couldn't see through it to the person who'd screamed and thrown it, though.

Over her shoulder, she asked Ken, "What's that supposed to do?"

The silence made her turn to look at him. He was scowling at the sparkly purple extinguisher fog, his mouth hanging open.

"You might want to close your mouth if that stuff is dangerous," she commented.

She wasn't sure it would get over or past her to him. She might well be protecting him from his own trap at the moment. Her powers were weird that way. But since she wasn't sure, she figured the reminder to not breathe it in might be good.

"What are you?" he hissed at her.

Ha! Well, at least he realized who was blocking the stuff this time. With an actual couple of witches in her group, she'd been sure one of them would get credit for this.

"You're a witch, too?" he asked, still staring at the purple fog.

She gave him a vague sort of shrug that didn't answer the question. "What's it supposed to do?" she asked again.

"I think it's supposed to…contain us," Angie answered. Her eyes were narrowed to slits as she studied the still hovering fog sand. "An… encasing spell if I'm reading it right."

Teresa let a long breath out through her nose. Just shy of a snort. She sounded irritated. "That could have gotten me, you idiot," she said to Ken.

"You don't think that was the point?" Cary said. She shook her head at both of them. "You're both very bad at this."

Angie, still studying the fog, said, "They'd probably be better at it if you weren't here."

"Na. I'm sure you'd have come up with something. You *are* good at this."

"Thank you," Angie said, flashing Cary a quick smile.

"You're welcome." Cary smiled back. "Now, what do we do about all this?"

The fog stuff—encasing spell whatever the hell that was— continued to hang in the air, dust motes in the gloomy corridor. Technically, Cary could just keep standing here and they'd be safe from the spell, but if it didn't dissipate or…something soon, it might continue to be dangerous after they left.

"Do we leave it and go get Ava, or…?"

Angie let out a long breath. "Probably better not leave it." She leaned to one side a little, as if attempting to look around the fog to the person who'd thrown it. "You caught in this now or can you call it back?" she asked.

A male voice said, "I…I don't know."

Cary hung her head. She glanced up at Teresa. "How did they get your niece? These guys aren't as competent as you led me to believe."

Teresa looked back and forth between Ken and the purple fog. "They're usually better at…"

"At what? Ken's face gives him away every time. They obviously don't know enough about magic to actually deal with it when something goes wrong. And they're looking to call a demon to get rid of mobsters —which, I have to say, is *not* an improvement on their situation with the mobsters." She tisked at Ken over her shoulder before facing Teresa again. "How did they get around you to get to your niece?"

She'd had the impression, from both Teresa and Angie, that Teresa was skilled in this revenge and deception stuff. Case in point, Cary hadn't expected her to be luring Angie here because this was a specific trap for Angie—for some weird reason to do with demons that needed to be part of a conversation later.

Although, to be fair, they had thought it was a trap, which was why Cary and the girls were here.

That reminded her. She pulled her phone out of the sealed side pocket on her leather jacket. It was sealed with magic so she wouldn't lose things like her phone and keys when jumping around protecting people. That had happened a lot in the first few months on this job. Marianne had sorted her out with the jacket.

She sent a quick text to Lucy and Marianne's phones: *You both okay?*

Lucy: *Fine. It's quiet.*

Marianne: *How you both doing?*

Cary: *Holding off some purple fog. Wondering why the bad guys are so bad at this.*

Lucy: *You have all the fun.*

Cary snorted and put her phone away. "All's quiet outside," she told Angie.

"Give me a sec, and I'll see if I can do something about the encasing spell. Doesn't look like it'll just fade." She shook her head. "Pretty short sighted, whoever designed that."

"The best witch we could find," Ken said, sounding less sure than he probably wanted to.

"Your 'best' wasn't so much," Angie said, then started murmuring quietly.

Cary recognized the Latin, which thrilled her—yay, she knew something!—but she couldn't decipher the spell Angie was reciting.

She'd have to ask her afterward what it was. Jaxer would want her to study this and learn.

After a few moments, the fog started to swirl, condensing and gathering in on itself, forming into a basketball-sized sphere. The sphere continued to hang in the air, but now Cary could see around it.

"Cool," she said to Angie. "What'd you do? Jaxer would want me to check," she added.

"A containment spell for the encasing spell," Angie said with a quick grin. "A sort of specialized containment circle that encircled the entire mass."

"Ah. Makes sense. Will it just stay there? Do we have to worry about breaking the containment?"

"We should avoid touching it," Angie said. "My spell is really specific to hold the magic *in* not keep anything out."

Meaning if they "crossed" the circle—or sphere in this case—they'd break it. Containment circles were cool witchy things that could hold stuff in, or out, depending on the spell. The one that circled Angie's house was designed to keep stuff out, at least as far as Cary knew. But keeping stuff inside from getting out *and* stuff from outside getting in, that was a trickier kind of spell. And probably took a lot longer to form when the thing you were trying to keep in was rogue magic.

"This'll do," she said. To Teresa, "Don't touch the purple fog basketball unless you want to get caught in the spell."

"I figured that out," Teresa said dryly.

"Don't get huffy with me," Cary said. "You're the one who got us into this." To the man she could now see standing behind the purple fog, she said, "Don't try to touch it. You'll unleash the spell on yourself."

He was a taller man, taller than Ken anyway, with skinny shoulders and a long face Cary would call distinctive if she wanted to be kind. That sort of face got called "horsey" on women, though, which kind of ticked her off. Also, she wasn't inclined to be kind to him, so she mentally thought of his face as a bit horsey. But then that seemed insulting to horses, and she liked horses, so she went back to distinctive, but with a definite irony to the thought.

He blinked at her a few times before refocusing on the swirling ball, his mouth hanging open. He hadn't spoken much, and he didn't look like he had much to say still.

"Can we get Ava now?" Teresa asked, interrupting Cary's silent contemplations.

She turned her attention on Teresa again. "Well, I don't know, do I? I mean, they could decide throwing more purple fog is a good idea. Or something else." She looked at Ken. "You got something else up your sleeve? Some other gotcha trick you want to explain to me?"

"What?" He shook his head and looked away from the swirling purple.

His expression went through a series of emotions, most of which looked like confusion and panic from the outside. Then he tried to school his features and give her a knowing smirk.

Cary rolled her eyes at him and looked at Angie. "So, Ava still behind Ken somewhere?"

"She is," Angie confirmed.

"All right then. Forward it is."

9

*C*ary faced the still-attempting-to-smirk-and-failing Ken. "You gonna move or just stand there and let my shield push you backward?"

"I'm not some easy pushover," Ken said.

"Sure, sure." She stepped forward and let her shield push him backward down the hall.

He stumbled a little before righting himself and pretending he'd meant to move backward.

"Which room?" she asked Angie.

"Not sure now." She scanned the three doors branching off the corridor. Then looked at the bend in the hallway that could either lead to another set of stairs or a fourth room. "Think I'll just touch some doorknobs."

"Good plan. Unless there's a gotcha spell on any of them."

Angie nodded at Ken. "He'd have let us know that by now. They didn't think of it." She glanced at Teresa. "And they weren't told to attempt it."

Teresa's expression didn't change.

Cary kept herself between the doors and Angie as Angie reached around to touch the knobs. She wasn't sure if this would protect Angie from spells in the doorknobs, but she knew if the door open she'd be able to protect her from whatever was beyond at least.

Ken pressed his hands against her shield, seemingly looking for a way around it. She mostly ignored him. She glanced at his associate once, but the "distinguished" faced guy was still staring at the purple fog basketball. He seemed reluctant to move around it. Which was handy since it meant he wasn't a problem Cary had to worry about just yet.

Angie grunted and nodded to the next door down the hall, across from the first. They moved to that one as a group and repeated the process.

Teresa's gaze moved between Ken and Angie, but her expression was carefully shuttered. Cary wanted to ask more questions. But she didn't want to disturb Angie's concentration so she held her tongue.

Angie shook her head and they moved on to the third door, once again crossing the hall. At this door, Ken's eyes grew wider and he rushed toward it, a pointless attempt to get between Angie and the door.

Cary shook her head at him when he got forced back a few feet. "You're a very slow learner," she said.

"Ava's not in there," Ken hissed. "You're not getting her until you cooperate."

Cary gave him a look. "Of course we are. Haven't you been paying attention?"

Angie hissed a curse and dropped her hand from the doorknob, then turned a glare on Ken. "You are such an asshole."

"What what?" Cary asked. "I mean, I already know he's an asshole. But what specifically did you see?"

Before Angie could answer, Cary's cellphone vibrated in her pocket. She pulled it out to see a text from Marianne.

Marianne: *Got company out here.*

"Shit." Cary showed the text to Angie.

Cary: *You need us?*

Marianne: *We got it. Mundanes.*

Okay, well that was maybe a good thing. Marianne would have

tricks mundane humans wouldn't have the skills to combat. And Lucy could kick the ass of mundane humans up and down the street without much trouble.

She showed the response text to Angie.

Angie nodded. "We'll get Ava and then go help."

"Who's here?" Cary asked Ken as they moved toward the bend in the hallway.

Ken frowned and glanced out toward the front of the house. "What are you talking about?"

"Brilliant," Cary said. "Just…great. These are probably the mob guys or something, huh? Someone you owe money to? You are *so* bad at this."

Ken looked toward the stairway and his associate still standing behind the purple sphere. "Go check it out," he barked.

The guy nodded and started toward the stairs.

"No," Teresa said. "I think you should stay where we can see you." She swatted the air and the purple basketball flew into the man's back. The contact with him broke Angie's containment spell and unleashed the encasing spell, which proceeded to encase the man in a soft purple glow. He froze in place, one foot lifted to start down the stairs.

Angie frowned at Teresa but didn't say anything.

"Telekinesis or a spell?" Cary asked.

Teresa smirked.

Angie said, "Telekinesis."

"Interesting." Cary nodded. "At least he won't be bothering Marianne and Lucy."

"What the hell have you done?" Ken's voice rose. "If it's them, they'll kill me."

"Them who?" Cary asked, just to be irritating.

She'd keep *them* whoever they were from killing Ken—despite herself, because it's just what she did—but she hated having to protect bad guys. And since she already felt like she was doing that with Teresa, and also that Ken brought this trouble on himself, she was really annoyed she might have to protect him.

She was sure Marianne and Lucy would handle the people outside, though. Which gave her and Angie time to rescue Ava and get out of there.

"Things are getting complicate," she said to Angie.

"Yup," Angie said and continued toward the bend in the corridor.

From outside, Cary heard the sound of someone scream, but it sounded like a male someone so she didn't immediately panic.

Cary: *You still okay?*

Marianne: *Good. Lucy broke someone's leg. His own fault.*

Cary: *Fair enough.*

"What was that?" Ken demanded even as he continued backing into the corridor bend.

"My friend broke someone's leg," Cary said. "Apparently, it was his own fault."

"Lucy?" Angie asked. Cary nodded, and Angie grinned. "They always underestimate her."

They reached the bend in the corridor. A closed door set back in a little recess. Not another hallway, just a deeper recess. Weird construction. But what did Cary know? She hadn't been inside many upscale houses like this. Maybe pointless recessed doors was the rage now.

Ken had backed himself against the door and was pinned between it and Cary's shield now. He was looking frantically around, but for what Cary couldn't tell. An escape? A weapon?

"If you run away," she said, "whoever's on your front lawn is probably coming after you. You'd be better staying put. Although, I am going to have to ask you to move out of the way so we can get to Ava."

"He's still got at least one other guy around here," Angie reminded her.

"And probably some nasty spells on the other side of that door," Teresa said.

"Well those would be bad to trigger right now, wouldn't they?" Cary said. "I mean, with him being in the way and all." She grinned as Ken's eyes widened.

Teresa reached forward and made a turning motion with her hand.

The doorknob wobbled. Ken's eyes widened further but when the door didn't open, he let out a breath and attempted to gloat.

The smirk wasn't nearly as effective as it might have been had he not been sweating through his shirt.

"Locked, stupid bitch," he said to Teresa. "You think I'm stupid?"

"Actually, I do," Teresa said. "And racist. And a crook. And you're gonna reap what you've sown."

"But not before we get her niece back," Angie said, her tone neutral.

"That last part in particular," Cary said. "Ava first. Sowing what you reap later."

"You'll have to get through me," Ken said. "Until the demon witch agrees to help me, the bitch's niece remains at my mercy."

Cary sighed. "You really really haven't been paying attention."

Another shout from outside, a very loud curse, silence.

Huh. Cary wondered what Marianne and Lucy were getting up to.

"Should I check on them again?" she asked Angie.

"They'll yell if they need help."

She supposed that was true. She nudged forward until Ken was forced back so tight against the door he looked smooshed.

She made a face. "You could just move," she said.

Then she reached around him and opened the door.

The lovely thing about Protector magic was that it gave her what she needed when she needed it. Mostly, all she needed was to just stand where she was and let the bad guys wear themselves out. But occasionally, she had to do more. Now this didn't extend to *actual* magic usage. Outside of channeling her bosses' magic, she couldn't do anything that would be considered offensive magic. She was a strictly defensive weapon.

But she could get a speed boost. Or fire a gun even though she hated them and never handled them if she could help it. Or she could dodge a knife and disarm someone if it came down to that—though it rarely did because standing still and letting themselves wear out was usually easier. Occasionally, the magic gave her... She thought of it as a little boost of strength. She could break through magic things, including spells.

And she could open locked doors.

Ken's eyes widened. And then he fell backward into the room, landing on his ass.

She'd have laughed if the room beyond hadn't contained a woman, sitting on a chair, and a man behind her holding a gun to her head.

Cary really hated guns.

10

_T_he woman in the straight-backed, wooden chair was young. Maybe twenty. Maybe not quite there yet. She had long black hair pulled into a thick braid, and a round, pretty face. Cary could see the familial resemblance to her aunt, but Ava's eyes weren't nearly as hard and cagey. In that moment, in fact, she looked scared.

Her captors had tied a gage around her mouth, which for some reason bothered Cary as much as the thick ropes strapping the young woman to the chair.

Ken scrambled up from his sprawl on the floor and straightened his shirt with a quick jerk. "As you can see," he said. "No's leaving until we deal." He pointed at Teresa, then Angie, and finally Cary. "And he will shoot her before you can stop it if you try anything funny."

Cary narrowed her eyes. With the gun so close to Ava, she wouldn't have time to get across the room and in between the woman and the bullet in time to stop it. And jumping to save Ava would leave Angie vulnerable. And Teresa. Although Cary was less worried about Teresa. She'd gotten her niece into this mess. Cary's sympathies for her were low.

"Ideas?" she murmured to Angie.

"Considering some things," Angie said.

"Don't," Ken hissed. "There's nothing you can do. We will kill her."

More noise from outside drew all their attention. This sounded like a window crashing. Cary winced. She wanted to go help Marianne and Lucy, too. Not being able to be in three places at once was sometimes a real pain in the ass.

"Your…friends?—" Cary raised her brows at Ken, "—friends outside are getting the crap beat out of them, but *if* they get through my friends, and into your house, I suspect it will not end well for you. I suggest you let us have Ava back, then we can go shoo the mob guys away. And you can reconsider all your life choices that got you to this point."

"They'll just come back," Ken said. "I need that demon."

Cary sighed. "Loopholes, Ken. There are always loopholes with demons. They're as bad as mob guys. Worse. Mob guys are more straightforward. You pay them back or they break something on you. Or maybe kill you eventually. Demons will play with your head and then eat you while you're still alive. Will mob guys eat you while you're still alive, Ken? I don't think so."

She heard Angie murmuring very quietly behind her, so she kept up a steady stream of chatter—which seemed to be her forte in these situations. Teresa moved to one side a little more and Cary sensed her coming up on her toes, as if preparing to move. While she talked, Cary also kept her gaze on the gun at Ava's head. When that shifted away from Ava, Cary could move. She'd have to trust Angie to keep herself safe in the interim. Teresa? Cary had a feeling the woman was used to taking care of herself.

At the moment, Cary's biggest concern, beyond keeping her own friends safe, was getting between Ava and any guns in the room.

"So you see, Ken," she said, "demons are just bad news. And a pain in the ass. And really why did you go to mob type people anyway? Don't you watch movies? TV? There've been some very good ones that go into great detail about why getting involved with mob guys is a really really bad idea. They could just shoot you because of a mood, Ken. Just because of a mood. And even then, that's still not as bad as what a demon might do to you. Do you want a demon owning your life, Ken? I wouldn't if I were you. See you have to rethink your life, Ken."

"Do you ever shut *up*?" Ken shouted.

"No. Not when lecturing someone on why summoning demons is a bad idea. I mean, really. It's a stupid idea, and I can't believe this has to be said out loud, but here we are."

The man holding the gun to Ava's head snickered, a sound he tried to muffle. Ken glared at him. The man shrugged. "She's funny."

"You think this is funny?" Ken snarled.

"That is what he just said," Cary said. "Thank you by the way," she said to the gun man. "Any chance I'm funny enough you'll move that gun and let us get Ava without anyone getting hurt?"

"No," the man said with another shrug. "But I like the way you irritate him."

"Fair enough." She went back to irritating Ken because from the corner of her eyes, she saw Angie's hands moving. "Now, here's the thing about demons, Ken. They are smart. Even the dumb ones are kind of smart. Cunning maybe is a better word. Cunning? Yeah, that's the one. And they are *very* motivated to get out of their own realms. Not really sure why. Outside of the realms being, you know, filled with demons. I've never been to one myself, so I can't say for sure, but I get the impression they're not nice places to be, sometimes even for a demon."

"They're not," Teresa said.

Which was a very interesting observation, and Cary desperately wanted to ask her how she knew, but figured she could ask later. "See. Bad places. But also, demons are motivated to get here because of all the human meat just walking around. Like walking into a candy store for a demon, Ken. A *candy* store. And if that doesn't motivate you, I don't know what will."

She watched Ken's head metaphorically explode and had to keep her grin contained. She'd been able to practice her "irritate the bad guy" ploy a lot over the last few years, and she was getting good at it, if she did say so herself.

Angie stopped murmuring, and Cary braced for whatever she was about to do, her gaze remaining firmly on the man with the gun even as she continued to ramble to Ken. Her ability to ramble nonsensically while paying attention to other things had improved over the last year, too. Though she felt like she could use more practice with that.

A few moments passed, nothing happened. And then the man with the gun hissed in a breath and started swatting at his bicep on his non-gun arm. He stumbled back three steps as he patted his arm and tried to move his long shirt sleeve out of the way so he could see his arm.

Cary moved the second the gun shifted away from Ava's head. She dove forward before Ken or the gunman could blink, and, thanks to Protector magic—yay magic!—she reached Ava just seconds before the gunman noticed she'd moved, raised his gun...

And fired.

11

At close range, when Cary was in the middle of getting between bad guys and good guys, bullets didn't have a lot of time to slow down.

She hissed as the first bullet hit her shoulder. That would leave a bruise. It didn't penetrate, of course, it just smashed into a flat and useless lump and fell to the ground. The next two shots fired did stop in time because once in place, the shields did a very good job of that sort of thing. Those two bullets also fell as useless lumps to the hardwood floor with little plinking noises.

Once she was sure she had Ava safe, she looked up at Angie. Angie flicked her fingers at the gunman again. His rather colorful curse proceeded the sound of something heavy hitting the floor.

Teresa dove toward the floor at the same time Ken did, but Teresa was on the correct side of the chair where Cary shielded Ava. Ken got knocked sideways. Teresa picked up the dropped gun.

"Well, that was fun," Cary murmured. She gently removed the gag in Ava's mouth. "You okay?" she asked as she went to work on the ropes.

"Not hurt," the young woman said, swallowing visibly. "What's happening?"

"Long story. We got you. You're safe now. We'll get out of here in just a minute." She fumbled with the knots, which were not yielding to her clumsy attempts to untie them, so she let out a breath, took hold of a section of rope in both hands, and pulled. Hard.

The rope ripped apart like thin cloth. Protector magic was very handy sometimes.

She shoved and unwrapped the rope until she had Ava free. Ken and the gunman had both, at Teresa's urgings, moved back against the wall. Angie joined Cary.

"What'd you do?" Cary asked her as she helped Ava stand.

"Little fire spell," Angie said. "They're tricky when dealing with someone holding a gun. Don't want them to accidentally pull the trigger. Can't burn them too close to the gun or the gun might explode." She shrugged. "I figured high on the arm not holding the gun would be enough distraction."

"Perfect," Cary said with a nod.

"You hurt?"

"One bruise. I'll be fine. I do hate getting shot, though."

"How did you get shot and aren't on the ground bleeding?" Ava asked. Her voice was soft and still sounded a little dry.

Cary waved her question away. "Just a knack for this kind of thing. No biggie. Shall we leave the men to the mobsters outside?"

"No!" Ken shouted. "You can't. You have to protect me."

"No I don't," Cary said. Although, she was a little afraid she might have to since it was her job, that she got paid for, and sometimes even rotten bad guys needed protecting. Although she always always hated when that happened.

"I can't even believe I have to say the word mobster," she continued. "That's just ridiculous. Who the hell gets themselves mixed up with mobsters these days? And then wants to summon a *demon* to solve the problem." She huffed out an irritated breath. "Ken, you really need to rethink your life choices. They have not been good."

Teresa raised the gun and cocked the hammer. Cary snarled and got between her and Ken and his associate.

She pointed at Teresa. "No. Hand that gun to Angie, or I'm leaving you behind to deal with the mob guys, too."

"Aunt Terry," Ava said quietly, holding her aunt's gaze. "Let's go. Let's go."

Teresa exchanged a look with her niece. A long look Cary was sure conveyed a lot of information. And she wasn't entirely sure that was a good thing. But right now, her priority was getting everyone out of this alive.

Teresa looked back at Ken, the gun still firmly pointed at him. "You endangered my family."

"You've been ruining my business," Ken said.

"You have an evil business."

"Look who's talking."

"What does that mean?" Cary asked.

"The demon," Ken said. "That was her idea. She swore one would help. She told me where to find the…men I could borrow money from. Then when I got in too deep, she promised the demons would help. But I couldn't summon them, and it was her fault."

"I'm not sure that's the scathing indictment you mean for it to be," Cary said, but she gave Teresa a narrow-eyed look.

"She wouldn't give me the final clue, the final thing I needed to complete the summoning. She refused, said it was my own fault because I wasn't offering the demons enough to lure them here. But I did my research. I knew she'd left something out."

"Which was why you kidnapped Ava?" Cary asked. Boy, she loved a good bad-guy-monologue. So enlightening.

"To get the last clue," Ken said, his lip lifted in a snarl. "She said I needed the witch."

"Well, obviously, you've been lied to, Ken," Cary said reasonably. "A lot. Which I believe makes you a…sucker, right? That's the word. Sucker. Like all the people you've stolen from in the past." She glanced at Teresa. "Hand Angie the gun. Now."

Teresa wavered a moment more and then, reluctantly handed the gun to Angie, hand grip first. Angie, with an ease that surprised Cary, dropped the magazine out of the gun and removed the bullet in the chamber, tucking the bullets and magazine into her jeans pocket and the gun into her coat pocket. She held Teresa's gaze for a moment afterward, another silent exchange there.

Cary's phone vibrated. She pulled it out. "Text from Marianne. They've chased off the bad guys, but all the ruckus attracted attention and the cops are pulling up outside." She looked at Angie. "We'd better go."

"No." Ken took a step forward. "You can't leave me. They'll be back."

Angie made a hand gesture and tossed it at Ken and the gunman who'd finally stopped patting his arm. A wall of blue fire rose up in front of the men, glowing faintly but without any heat.

"What's that?" Cary asked.

"Containment wall. It'll keep them for a few minutes and be gone by the time the cops come up."

"No!" Ken rushed the wall. The blue flames hissed as he hit them, and he screamed, falling away from the wall, shaking out his hands.

He wasn't on fire, but touching the blue wall sounded to Cary like it had hurt.

"Rethink your life choices, Ken," Cary repeated as she ushered the women ahead of her so she could keep Ken and the gunman behind her, just in case they decided to risk the blue fire wall again.

<h1 style="text-align:center">12</h1>

"We should probably do something with that gun," Cary murmured to Angie as they headed out of the house. She considered the still-frozen man at the top stair as they passed him. His eyes were wide but other than that, he was perfectly still with the slight purple glow around him. "Should we…do something about him?" she asked.

"It'll wear off in a few more minutes," Angie said. "Probably."

"The cops are gonna wonder what he's doing."

"I'm sure Ken will come up with some excuse," Teresa said. "He's good at convincing people of things."

"I do not get that," Cary said on the way down the stairs. "He seems too obvious and stupid."

"You'd be surprised what people fall for," Ava said quietly.

Cary couldn't see Ava's expression so she couldn't know for sure, but she got the impression there was a double meaning in that comment.

She shook that off and at the bottom of the stairs, moved into the lead of the group. If the cops had twitchy trigger fingers, or the mob guys came back, she wanted to be out front to keep everyone safe.

Also, she was never going to get over the fact that there had been actual mobsters here. It was something out of a movie. Yes, she dealt with vampires, and shapeshifters, and wizards, and witches. But mobsters? That was just weird.

Just before stepping out, Angie said to Teresa, "We're going to tell the police that Ken conned Ava to get her here, and we came to get her back. That he's a conman, that the people Lucy and Marianne fought were here for Ken, and that they need to investigate him."

"They won't," Teresa said. "He'll talk his way out of it. He'll bribe someone. Or know someone. Or have someone in his pocket."

"Fine. Then he'll have to take his chance alone with the mobsters. Or finish calling a demon himself and die that way. But we're going to tell the cops as much of the truth as we can, and then we're leaving. And you will not drag me into this shit ever again."

Angie held Teresa's gaze for a long time. Cary looked between them, desperately wanting to ask questions. There was a lot there. History. And anger.

"You need to stop messing with demon stuff, too," Angie said more quietly. "I know you didn't intend for him to be able to summon one. At least there's that this time around. But even implanting the idea is stupid and you know it. He was attempting a summoning in that room. He could have figured it out eventually. May still."

"And then he'll die," Teresa said. "I won't be terribly upset about that."

"And if the demon gets out and kills more people than just Ken? Kills innocent people? Or Ken sacrifices someone innocent?"

"That's what the demon hunters are for, right?" Teresa said, with a sneer.

"If they don't get there in time? Or die?" Angie snarled the last. "Enough of this. After all these years, enough. You nearly got your niece killed this time. And for what? The off chance the cops will finally investigate? Or he'll get himself killed? You could do so much more with your life, Teresa."

"This is my life. And I don't answer to you."

Angie let out a long breath. "But eventually you will answer to someone. The scales will balance and a reckoning will come. Who will you lose when that happens?"

Without waiting for an answer, Angie turned toward the front door and motioned for Cary to open it. Cary didn't hesitate, but the exchange left her extremely curious. The look that passed between Ava and her aunt, the way Teresa lifted her chin almost defiantly at her niece's expression… That was interesting, too.

Outside, they found Marianne standing near the door, her hands carefully *not* in her purse. Lucy stood on the sidewalk surrounded by four male cops, all of whom were about a foot or more taller than her. But where Cary had been fearing handcuffs, and was going to rush forward to intervene, what she saw gave her pause.

"Is she showing them self-defense moves?" Cary quietly asked Marianne.

Marianne snorted. "She's *teaching* them proper form for some moves. Girl cannot stop teaching."

"And they're listening?"

"Intently. Also making eyes at her. I think that short cop has seen his own personal miracle—and she's a five-foot-tall redhead in a gi."

Cary pressed her lips together so she wouldn't laugh.

"Do we need to explain things?" Angie asked, her tone quiet.

Marianne glanced at her. "Lucy's got it handled. She spun a tail of men trying to mug her and not realizing they'd attacked a martial arts instructor. She played the pretty woman card and batted her eyelashes, and somehow that segued into what she's doing now. It was as impressive a display of 'handling the situation' as I've ever seen."

"Neither of you were hurt?" Cary asked.

"No, we're good. Lucy got to have fun tossing a few grown men around. Though one of them was pretty pissed when she threw his associate onto his car and shattered the front window. And the two I handled will…find their way out of the oubliette eventually. I left them rope."

"Will they survive that effort?" Cary asked.

"Sure. So long as they don't piss off the troll that lives nearby."

"Looks like my friends have saved you some explaining," Angie said to Teresa.

Teresa didn't comment.

Ava, however, said, "Thank you. All of you. For coming to rescue me."

"It's what we do," Cary said.

Although, really, they didn't have to go do things like this hardly ever. Still, it did occasionally come up.

"I know it wasn't..." She glanced at her aunt. "There were complications involved. Thank you for overlooking them."

Cary and Marianne both watched Angie's response to that. Angie just nodded, making no other comment.

Lucy finished dealing with the cops, giving her phone number to the short one before he left.

Marianne shook her head at Lucy as she walked back up the steps to join them at the house. "A cop? You really going to date a cop?"

Lucy shrugged. "We'll see. I gave him my business number, not my cellphone. Just in case."

Marianne smirked. Lucy grinned back.

"We're all done here," Angie said quietly. "I'd like to get back to my family now. I don't want my parents worried."

"What about...?" Cary nodded toward the house. The three bad guys were still in there, even if one was still frozen and the other two were behind a magic firewall. Plus, Angie still had their gun in her pocket.

Angie took out the gun even as Cary thought of it, and to Marianne said, "You have anything in your purse to get rid of this?"

Marianne considered the gun. "Sure." She dug around a bit and then pulled out a piece of wispy, blue-colored cloth that looked as light and insubstantial as a cloud. "Set it on the ground."

Angie did as instructed, putting the magazine and extra bullet next to the gun.

Marianne held the cloth over the gun a moment, then dropped it, letting it drift down. Despite how light the material looked, it didn't float away in the breeze or shift directions. It dropped directly onto the gun, settling into a flat little square. When Marianne picked it up again, the gun was gone.

"Where'd it go?" Lucy asked.

"Middle of nowhere." Marianne glanced at Cary when Cary opened her mouth. "But not the oubliette," she assured. "I like that troll."

"Fair enough." Cary glanced at the house. "And the bad guys?"

"Let them rot," Teresa said.

"They'll come after you again," Angie said. "Maybe Ava."

Ava straightened her shoulders a little but didn't otherwise comment.

"I'll take care of this from here," Teresa said.

"Don't get your niece killed," Angie said. "Do *not* call any demons. And don't come to me for help again. Especially when it's under the guise of offering me up as a sacrifice."

"I knew you were a match for them," Teresa said, sounding almost petulant.

"You offered to sell me out in exchange for your niece. Lying to them or not, I didn't appreciate the surprise. Or the deception. Don't contact me again. Ever."

"You don't miss it?" Teresa asked, her eyes narrowed.

"Not even a little bit," Angie said.

They watched Teresa and Ava drive off safely, ensuring Ken didn't come out of the house and try to attack them again, and were heading back to Marianne's car before Cary finally asked Angie, "Demon witch? What did they mean by calling you that?"

Angie shook her head. "Long story. I can't really talk about it now."

"One day?"

"Maybe. What I can. But now, I'd rather go eat Mexican food with my family. You guys want to join us? Seems the least I can do after all your help." She wagged her eyebrows. "My dad makes a mean pulled pork taco."

"I'm in," Lucy said without hesitating. "Between my classes and the fight here, I'm starving."

"I could eat," Marianne said. "Let me text Gina so she knows not to expect me for dinner."

"She can join us too," Angie said, opening the passenger-side door of Marianne's car.

"I'll let her know," Marianne said, her face in her phone as she texted her girlfriend and climbed into the driver's seat at the same time. "She's working but when she gets off her shift at the bar, she might be hungry."

As Cary slid into the back seat, she glanced in the direction of Ken's house and wondered if maybe she should…warn someone about him. Maybe her bosses. Or Jaxer. Or maybe they could find a demon hunter and warn them to keep an eye on Ken.

She hoped Teresa and, especially, Ava left Ken alone, though. She hoped this didn't spill back over into Angie's life. She hoped Ken got some sort of consequences for his actions one day, but that those consequences didn't come at the cost of innocent lives.

Angie glanced over the front seat at Cary and said, "I'll text someone. Don't worry. Ken won't be able to hurt anyone in his demon quest."

Cary felt her shoulders relax. "Thanks. How did you know I was worrying about that?"

"You're a Protector," Angie said with a smile that looked significantly more relaxed than any expression she'd had since Teresa showed up at her house. "You can't help yourself. Worrying about people's safety is how you got your job."

Cary snorted.

Well if that wasn't the damned truth.

THANK YOU

Thank you for reading Witches and Weavers and Ghosts, Oh Boy! I hope you enjoyed the collection and each of the novellas exploring more history and background for each of Cary's best friends. As I mentioned in the introduction, I loved writing these stories. I hope they were as fun for you to read as they were for me to write.

For more Cary Redmond adventures, don't miss the main series, starting with The Trouble with Black Cats and Demons. There are also a lot more Cary Redmond short stories available. If Angie's story piqued your interest, her series starts with the short story *Moonlit Strange*, and the first novel Bone Lantern Witch.

For more on my books, new releases, updates, exclusive excerpts, and the occasional free story, join my newsletter (https://bit.ly/KatSimonsNewsletter). All new subscribers get a free, exclusive story in my Tiger Shifters Paranormal Romance universe. This story is only available to newsletter subscribers. It was originally written for an erotic romance anthology, though, so just a warning that it's…sexy.

If you'd prefer, you can get information about new releases and upcoming events at my website (https://www.katsimons.com), or follow my author page at your favorite vendors.

Thanks again for reading!

BOOKS BY KAT SIMONS

Cary Goes to Hawaii

Cary Holidays

Cary and Dragons and Goblins

Cary's Galentine's Day

When Cary Met the Good Guys (Collection 1)

Dates, Dinners, and Other Disasters (Collection 2)

Witches and Weavers and Ghosts, Oh Boy (Collection 3)

DEMON WITCH SERIES

Moonlit Strange

1 – Bone Lantern Witch

JOAN OF KERRY SERIES

1 – Joan of Kerry: Joan and the Abhartach

2 – Joan and the Leprechaun

HAUNTS AND HOWLS COLLECTIONS

Haunts and Howls and Guardian Spells

Tombstone Wizard

MORE BOOKS

ABOUT THE AUTHOR

Kat Simons earned her Ph.D. in animal behavior, working with animals as diverse as dolphins and deer. She brought her experience and knowledge of biology to her paranormal romance and urban fantasy fiction, where she delights in taking nature and turning it on its ear. Her Tiger Shifters series combines romance and the otherworldly with heart-pounding action adventure. Her latest urban fantasy romance series follows the adventures of Protector Cary Redmond as she tries to manage her personal life while saving the world. A lot.

For something a little different, Kat also publishes fantasy romance, science fiction romance, and the occasional hockey romance under the name Isabo Kelly (https://www.isabokelly.com).

After traveling the world, Kat now lives in New York City with her family. She is a stay-at-home mom and a full time writer.

For more on Kat and her future books:

Website: https://www.katsimons.com
Newsletter: https://bit.ly/KatSimonsNewsletter
Facebook Page: https://www.facebook.com/KatSimonsAuthor